THE CASE OF THE PERFECT ALIBI

THE CASE OF THE PERFECT ALIBI

Mark Carrel

CHIVERS
THORNDIKE

This Large Print book is published by BBC Audiobooks Ltd, Bath, England and by Thorndike Press®, Waterville, Maine, USA.

Published in 2004 in the U.K. by arrangement with Golden West Literary Agency.

Published in 2004 in the U.S. by arrangement with Golden West Literary Agency.

U.K. Hardcover ISBN 1–4056–3060–4 (Chivers Large Print)
U.S. Softcover   ISBN 0–7862–6840–9 (Nightingale)

The text of this Large Print edition is unabridged.
Other aspects of the book may vary from the original edition.

Set in 16 pt. New Times Roman.

Printed in Great Britain on acid-free paper.

British Library Cataloguing in Publication Data available

Library of Congress Control Number: 2004107516

CHAPTER ONE

Brewster slid into the booth with his eyes bouncing off the horde of faces in the bar-room. A hum of sound made stale air thicker in a poorly ventilated and shadowy lighted room. He put his hat on the table and gazed sceptically at the mareschino cherry floating half submerged in an amber drink before him. He looked up at Mike Karger's square, patient face and said: 'What's that?'

'Drink it and find out,' Karger said. 'I ordered something special for an old friend just returned to the city.' Karger jutted his chin. 'That's it.'

Brewster edged the glass away. 'The continental approach doesn't look good on you, Mike. Let's carve the meat. Why'd you call me?'

'The pitch is an old story; the angles are new.'

'Listen; you know I'm still—'

Karger bored in like he hadn't heard. 'The woman's name is Madison—Golda Madison.' He made a small gesture of distaste. 'I know— it's a God-awful name. Anyway, she was engaged to a bird named Patrick Mallory. You'll meet him; tall, crisp-haired athletic type, maybe thirty, maybe a shade over.'

'*Was* engaged?'

1

Karger looked pointedly at the highball glass. 'I thought that might keep you occupied long enough for me to finish,' he said.

'Excuse me. You're a little edgy, Mike. I think you need a vacation too.'

'All right; you've got the funny out of your system. I'll go on. Patrick Mallory—Golda Madison; they *were* engaged but she broke it off a year or so ago when she met Hugo Drexler.'

'You're sure taking the long way to the morgue—which one's dead?'

'Drexler. It's a natural situation for a guy like him, too. I ran a make on him. He's scuffled with the law a dozen times, each time on the high planes of illegality. Bucket-shops, market manipulations, stock brokerage—like that. One of those guys who deal in millions, usually other people's millions, and occasionally a little of it sticks to their fingers. An operator, in other words.'

'A pleasant change from muck-raking the tenderloin.'

'Very pleasant,' Karger said dryly. 'Instead of guns these people use brains and sometimes city cops aren't as well equipped with the latter as with the former.'

'Okay; who made Drexler dead?'

'Who? Why would I call you down here for a high-ball if I knew who? I know *what,* but not who.'

'*What,* then?'

2

'A very neat shot through the brisket. The body's over at the morgue. They'll finish with the post this afternoon and turn it over to next-of-kin. Calibre .32. The lab boys're digging the slug out of his wall now.'

'When did this happen?'

'Medical examiner says around six this morning, give or take an hour or so.'

'Before breakfast. Who spent the night with Hugo Drexler?'

Mike Karger's face registered disdain. 'I told you these people are upper class,' he said.

'The corpse could have had a wife, couldn't he? Besides, because they're on their uppers doesn't mean they aren't human.'

'Drexler was a bachelor, in the first place, and in the second place guys like Drexler don't get up before six o'clock, wife or no wife.' Karger tossed off the rest of his highball and let out a shuddering breath. The ebb and flow of humanity moving around the booth went unnoticed by him, just as the pale colour of the bar's clientele contrasted with Brewster's tanned, good-looking face. Karger spoke again.

'There's an odd wrinkle to this case, Paul. It's something that may or may not have significance. This Drexler, Golda and Pat Mallory went on a sort of picnic yesterday. Out in the country to some old Indian ruin. Drexler climbed to the top of the thing to see the view. Golda was downstairs resting—she says she fell asleep. Mallory told me he was exploring the lower level of the ruin. Golda was awakened by one hell of a yell. She rushed up the old steps and found Drexler'd tumbled off the top.'

'How far'd he fall?'

'Not far enough apparently. He was only bruised. Anyway, it spoilt the day so they went back to Drexler's place, had a few drinks and broke up.'

'Mallory took Golda home?'

'Yes. Now, after Drexler copped a slug I questioned Golda till hell froze over and for two days on the ice. She told me that on the ride back from the Indian ruin Mallory and Drexler did not speak to one another. Not a word. At Drexler's apartment Golda got uncomfortable and asked Mallory to take her home, which he did. I suspect from this something happened at the ruin which made the two men pretty angry at one another.'

'Drexler thought Mallory shoved him off the ruin,' Paul Brewster said, 'which Mallory may have done. Why? It's simple, Mike; Mallory had a heart-burn over Drexler beating his time with Golda. The next question is—what's Golda Madison got one man would try to kill another man over?'

'Nuts,' Karger said. 'Why would Mallory push Drexler off a wall so low it didn't even break his leg?'

'How did Mallory know it wouldn't kill him?

4

Suppose Drexler'd landed on his head or neck.'

'That's pretty weak,' Karger said, disgustedly. 'If a man premeditates murder, Paul, he uses better logic than that.'

'All right; let's let that pass for now. What about Golda Madison?'

'Standard female equipment only more of it and better proportioned than average, but that's not it—at least I don't think it is. She's got money. How much I don't know yet but from appearances I'd say enough to make her doggoned interesting to a single man, with or without money.'

'That'll hold Golda for the time being,' Paul Brewster said. 'Fill me in on Patrick Mallory.'

'I don't know much more than I've already said. The murder took place about dawn this morning and it's now—one-thirty. There's one thing I can tell you though, and that's why I asked you to meet me here; he couldn't have killed Drexler.'

'Be careful, Mike. I've seen some wonderful alibis busted wide open and so have you.'

'I'm being careful all right. He was at headquarters when Drexler was killed.'

Brewster leaned back. 'That's the best,' he said thoughtfully. 'In fact it's so good I'd say you're trying to pin something on Mallory that he didn't do.'

'Nuts! I'm not trying to pin this on anyone, all I'm trying to do is figure it out—and

5

eventually catch a killer.'

'Why was Mallory at headquarters so early in the morning?'

'Some slob stole his car. He was reporting it.'

Brewster inflated and deflated his cheeks, gave a big shrug and said, 'Mallory's down the drain as a suspect then. Did you verify that he *was* there?' Karger nodded solemnly. 'That makes Golda next then. Lord; what a name! What's her alibi?'

'The usual. She took a bath after Mallory left her, had a nap, ate dinner and retired. She's single—there's no one to verify the fact that she didn't leave her apartment. She told me she didn't arise until nine this morning.' Mike gestured with his hands. 'You can believe it or you can break it wide open. She can't prove she was at her apartment around six this morning because the maid doesn't show up until eight, but until you get something good you can't tie her to the murder, either.'

'Would she have a reason, Mike? I mean— she's got the hots for the guy so why kill him?'

'Why? Who knows why,' Mike said. 'Anyway, that's all of it.'

'I see. And I'm supposed to come in a day early to help you—right?'

'Right. It's strictly voluntary, Paul. By the way, how was the vacation?'

'Perfect, Mike. Fishing every day, dancing every night. Beautiful weather, lots of

6

glamour, swimming . . .'

'Tahoe,' Mike said. 'Did you go over to Reno?'

'Sure.'

'See any familiar faces at the dice tables?'

'I didn't look for any. I wasn't a cop, I was just another guy on his vacation.'

'You sure picked up a nice tan. Goes well with blue eyes.'

Paul lit a cigarette, tossed the pack on the table and gazed at it. 'Well; I'm back and this is the first case of the new year. I suppose you covered Drexler's apartment—is that where he stopped it?'

'I covered it like a dog hunting a lamp-post. There were prints galore and five will get you ten there isn't a one that'll help us. I also got his date book, his private files and bank statements. Got everything but a practical reason for his being knocked off.'

'But you think Pat Mallory had a hand in it.'

Mike took a cigarette from the packet, lit it and exhaled. 'I'd *like* to think that, but I don't see how he could've. Sure; there's the hired gun angle but somehow it doesn't fit—not with these people. The more I studied the thing this morning at breakfast the more I wanted to ask you to come in a day early.'

'That part's all right, Mike. You'd do as much for me. Besides, I'm a little fed up on inactivity.'

'Well, Paul, he may have done it. May have

7

done it over Golda. That's the way I'd like to make this case, but I just can't make it stick with that alibi, so now we've got to do some real digging.'

'Which should begin with Golda. If we can find a motive she'll fit the description.'

'Maybe she will. Maybe someone we don't know anything about did it. She's engaged to Drexler; there doesn't appear to be another woman; he has money and so has she—does it sound reasonable that she'd murder him?'

'No,' Paul said, 'but I've yet to see a reasoning murderer or a reasonable murder. But assuming there was a third party involved—what do we know about Drexler's friends and associates?'

'Nothing. It just happened this morning, remember.'

Paul stood up, looked casually at the people in the room and said, 'Are we on it right now?'

'Right now. Cap said to stay on it until we've got the killer. He also said if it wasn't cracked by the time for my vacation—no vacation.' Mike squeezed out of the booth, stood up and said, 'Nice guy, Captain Benton; they say his mother raised another litter after his.'

Brewster said nothing until they were outside on the sidewalk moving toward the two-tone police sedan at the kerb. 'If this Drexler was a sharp operator isn't it likely he had a run in with some syndicate or other?'

Mike slid into the auto on the driver's side

8

without comment, slumped in his rumpled suit, lit a cigarette and exhaled mightily. Beyond the windscreen a multi-coloured serpentine of traffic wound past in a murky stench of its own making.

'I thought of that,' he said. 'I guess the best way to determine its feasibility would be to talk to Golda; she'd know more about his dealings than anyone else, I suppose.' When Paul Brewster nodded Karger eased the car from the kerbing. 'She lives in one of those studio-apartments on Normandie. Two-one-two.'

They drove through town without a word passing between them until Mike braked before a French villa type apartment house obviously tenanted by people of substance. Mike got out and squinted at the smooth, creamy plaster.

'Upstairs. She's got the entire second floor and a maid as pretty as a picture and as Irish as Paddy's pig.'

Brewster followed Mike across a velvety lawn and into the patio, skirted an elaborate fishpond, feeling the peacefulness of the setting seeping into him. An exotic tree with shiny dark leaves and bizarre red flowers shaded the arched entrance. They climbed a short, antiqued flight of stone steps and Mike rapped on the first door they approached. The woman who appeared in the opening was striking; endowed with more than the usual

9

amount of attractiveness, she looked at Mike in recognition, then past him to Paul Brewster. Karger introduced his partner, entered the room and did not see the way Golda Madison's glance widened slightly and followed Brewster as he passed through the doorway.

'We would like to ask you a few more questions, Miss Madison,' Mike said.

'Certainly.' She motioned towards chairs. 'A little of the sense of unreality has worn off, Sergeant Karger.'

Paul appraised her from behind the facade of a professional smile. She was statuesque, taller than average but with a totally natural grace. Her features were mobile, their normal expression open, candid, and interested. Now a cloud lay upon them, but so gently as to not materially disturb the quiet confidence that lay underneath. Paul Brewster's conclusion that it would be entirely possible for one man to kill another over her, obvious wealth notwithstanding, put at rest earlier vague doubts. Her large grey eyes moved liquidly from Paul to Mike, when the older man dropped into a deep chair and emitted a grunt not dissimilar to the sound of a gratified pig in a puddle of cool mud.

'What can I tell you?'

Paul edged forward in his chair. 'Miss Madison, you told Sergeant Karger of a strained relationship between Mallory and

10

Drexler on the way back from your picnic yesterday. Can you add anything to it?'

She gazed at him very steadily. 'I don't know what I can add,' she said. 'It seemed to grow out of Hugo's fall off the wall out at that old ruin.'

'I see. Now, after Drexler fell, did you run out where he was?'

'Yes; he shouted or cried out as he fell. It awakened me and I ran outside, around the building to where he lay.'

'Where was Mallory?'

Her eyes flickered. 'Behind me somewhere. He came up a moment after I knelt beside Hugo.'

'How high was the wall Drexler fell off of?'

'I don't believe it's over twenty feet high.'

'Not high enough to cause death to someone falling off it?'

She hesitated over the answer. Her attention was directed fully towards Paul. 'Why no,' she said carefully. 'I wouldn't think so; not normally anyway. I suppose if a person landed in such a manner which would break their back . . .'

'Of course,' Paul said. 'And exactly what happened right after the fall?'

'Hugo's ankle was injured. Pat and I helped him up. We rested inside the ruin for a few minutes. Hugo made a bandage of his handkerchief, wrapped it very tightly about his ankle then Pat and I helped him down to the

11

car and Pat drove us to Hugo's. We had a drink at Hugo's apartment then Pat drove me home.'

'But before that—before you got to Drexler's—in what way did the two men seem antagonistic towards one another?'

Her brows drew down in a faint frown. 'Not antagonistic, exactly . . .'

'But they didn't speak—isn't that what you told Sergeant Karger?'

'Yes, but it was one of those things you *feel* rather than see.'

'But you were conscious of it?'

'Yes, I was conscious of it. They did not speak to each other on the way to Hugo's, but it wasn't so noticeable then—there was little to say really. At the apartment Hugo mixed a drink, handed it to me and neglected to fix Pat one; that was the first thing I noticed. Hugo wasn't like that; he was very courteous, very considerate, normally. Then—they spoke to me but not to each other. It made a very uncomfortable situation and when I could, I asked Pat to drive me home.'

'And you wondered about this veiled hostility?' She nodded, her glance lifting to Paul's face. 'Yes, I wondered about it.'

'You wondered if it didn't arise from some idea Drexler had that Mallory may have pushed him off that wall, didn't you?'

Another brief nod. 'Yes; but that's not very logical, Mr. Brewster. Why would Pat do it; I mean, assuming he intended to hurt—to kill—Hugo, why would he push him off a wall no higher than twenty feet? Certainly the odds against Hugo being fatally injured were very great—wouldn't you think?'

Paul said, 'It's puzzling all right. Now I'd like to ask you a personal question and I hope you understand why it's necessary.' Her grey eyes, candidly level with his, were lovely and a little disturbing.

'I won't mind,' she said, and the tone of her reply brought Mike Karger's glance up from the floor.

'You had broken your engagement to Patrick Mallory and were currently engaged to Hugo Drexler. Wasn't it—I mean—didn't it seem tactless to you to go on a picnic with both of them?'

She said, 'I told myself it wasn't—that we were mature people—but apparently it wasn't a good idea after all. But until Hugo's accident there was no undercurrent, Mr. Brewster. Hugo was pleasant when he picked us up and Pat, who has a very effervescent personality, was himself in every way. I didn't think anything about it until on the way back. That was when I decided I had made a mistake.'

'Was the picnic your idea?'

'No; it was Hugo's.'

'On the same personal level I'd like to ask why you broke your engagement to Mallory?'

She hung-fire a second over the answer,

13

then said, 'Well; our interests differed too much, that is all.'

Paul was silent, watching; waiting for something less vague. While he waited he sought flaws in her beauty and found none.

She looked down at her hands once, then back to Paul's face. Mike Karger became conscious of some unique tension in the room.

'That's not very definite is it?' she said.

Paul still did not speak. She looked at him steadily and a small, wry smile touched her lips. 'Pat is nice. He's very clever and very successful; he's wonderful to go out with but he's a little unstable at times; a little unreliable.'

A drunk or a woman-chaser; Paul nodded; he was conceiving a mental image of Patrick Mallory; it fitted a type he was not unfamiliar with. 'Now about Drexler—had you known him a long time before your engagement?'

'No, not too long.'

Paul stood up. 'Would you have married him, Miss Madison?' He expected an angry reply but she simply stood up across the room from him with a frank expression and held his gaze.

'I don't know, Mr. Brewster. I honestly can't say whether I would have or not. Why did you ask that?'

'Because you don't impress me as a person who is particularly broken up over their finance's murder, Miss Madison.'

14

She kept her eyes on him through the interval of silence while Mike Karger pushed himself up out of the chair and moved towards the door.

'One more question: Can you think of anyone who might wish Drexler dead?'

'No, but I'm sure Pat had nothing to do with it. They may have had a misunderstanding over Hugo's fall, but I know Pat—he wouldn't kill anyone; just wouldn't.'

'Or push him off that wall?'

'That's asinine, Mr. Brewster—give me one reason why; just one?'

Paul made a small smile. 'I just *ask* questions,' he said.

'Hugo fell, I'm convinced of that. As I said before, if Pat intended to—'

'We're straying from the question, Miss Madison. Who were Drexler's associates; his friends; did he have business enemies?'

She shrugged and glanced at Mike Karger at the door as though tired of the conversation. 'I knew very little about Hugo's activities. He wasn't a talkative man nor the type who makes confidants.'

'But you knew what he did for a living, didn't you?'

For the first time her expression became guarded. 'I only knew he was an investor,' she said.

'Do you own a gun, Miss Madison?'

'Yes. Would you like to see it?'

15

'What calibre is it?'

'I'll get it.'

He watched her leave the room then faced Karger. 'Where's the exotic maid?' Mike shrugged, jerked his head toward a door beyond the dining-room and did not speak. Paul gazed around the room. Two immense glass windows ran from ceiling to floor. They were narrow and without cross-members. Beyond lay the haze and the city, the soft beauty of early afternoon.

'She's beautiful, Mike.'

Karger nodded again, but that time he spoke. 'So's Drexler,' he said shortly.

'She didn't do it.'

'No,' Karger said in the same dour way. 'Not the type. I guess Lucrezia Borgia wasn't the type either, and by the way—she's not engaged at the moment—if you hurry you can still get in the line.'

Paul's eyes smouldered but Golda Madison came back into the room at that moment. She held a cardboard box out. Paul took it and looked inside at the tiny .25 automatic pistol of foreign manufacture with gold and silver overlay which nestled in the dark cloth of the box. The gun was artistically chased and quite apparently very expensive; it was also as utilitarian as two left legs. He closed the box and handed it back to her.

'Do you have a permit for it?'

'Permit? Why no; I thought as long as you

16

didn't take a gun out of your house you didn't need one. Aren't permits required only for carrying concealed weapons?'

Score for Golda, Paul thought saturninely; she must have been engaged to an attorney also, at some time. 'May I ask where you got it?'

'Pat Mallory gave it to me on my birthday two years ago.'

'Thanks. One more thing: Where is this ruin where you picnicked?'

'It's quite a way back in the hills beyond Sherwood Valley. We had to leave the car and walk a mile or so through brush and rocks to get there. I'm not sure I could describe the way up there; I'd never been there before.'

'Well; thank you, Miss Madison. We may have to contact you again.'

'You're quite welcome,' she said moving toward the door.

Mike stumped stolidly across the patio as far as the fishpond. There he stopped a moment, peering down at the clear water and waiting for Paul to come close. 'Want to go take a look at Drexler?'

'No; where's Mallory live?'

Mike resumed his way toward the police sedan without answering. When they were both in and he had started the engine, he gave a short, squirting little laugh. Paul turned sharply and looked at him.

'What was that for?'

17

'You and Golda; you two ought to form a mutual admiration society. I don't think she even knew I was in the room.'

Paul lit a cigarette and wagged his head ruefully. 'You sure do need a vacation,' he said. 'Okay; where's Mallory live?'

'Twelve Overstrom Road.' Mike sounded cheerful; like a man whose interest in life had been restored. 'You know, Paul, with her fortune and your five-fifty a month you wouldn't have to take turns making the television payments.'

Paul inhaled, exhaled, and stared at the growing snail of traffic. 'Hit the siren,' he said, and even his ears were red.

Mike touched the switch. A low growl began which ended in a deafening shriek and cars swerved out of their way. They broke clear of the traffic snarl and shot ahead with a wide expanse of pavement open in all directions. When Mike turned the siren off he was still wearing a lop-sided grin.

'I got a notion when she looks at you she's got a fish-hook in each eye.'

'Well,' Paul said brusquely, 'you're the kind of a sucker who recognises the best quality bait.'

Number Twelve Overstrom Road was an older house, set back amid a profusion of immaculate lawns and thick shrubbery. It looked as though it had never lacked for care, and neither did Patrick Mallory the Fourth,

18

resident owner, attorney at law and man about town, who opened the door under Mike's fist.

Mallory nodded and stepped aside. His face was totally blank and not particularly glad looking. 'Come in.'

Mike introduced Paul Brewster. They were the same size and build. Both were tanned although Mallory's face was beginning to show a faint suggestion of lines, indicating he was the older of the two. Mallory brushed Paul's hand without grasping it and waved them to chairs in a darkly panelled and richly appointed living-room.

'Turned up anything, Karger,' he said in an almost disinterested way, and following it with a slow and casual glance.

When Mike answered Paul used the same moment to make a raking appraisal of the furnishings of the house. They told him a lot about Patrick Mallory. Being educated to the law had been the means to an end; the end being law, the means being four sparkling years of university life. Mallory had money; had obviously inherited it since, at thirty-five or thereabouts, he could hardly have amassed all which now surrounded him and which very obviously was wealth.

A plethora of pictures indicated that once at any rate Pat Mallory had been quite an athlete. Now of course he was a little soft appearing. Still, the muscle-tone was still in evidence; the perfect timing of movement and co-ordination.

When Mike's reply died away Paul said, 'Do much fishing, Mr. Mallory?'

Mallory looked blank. 'Fishing? No, never did much, why?'

'Just wondered. Looks like you were an all-round sportsman during college.'

'Oh. I went out for some sports, yes, but fishing wasn't one of them.'

'Do you like to hunt?'

'Occasionally, but I've about arrived at the conclusion you have to do too much walking any more for the shots you get. A case of too little game and too many hunters.' He was looking at Paul with curiosity plain in his face. 'I don't believe I've ever met you before, Mr. Brewster. Odd too, because from time to time I've met most of the local detectives.'

Paul didn't let the conversation get away from him. 'How about skeet and target shooting. Do any of that?'

'No,' Mallory said, the genial tolerance atrophying a little, his blue eyes chilling over in a defensive and antagonistic way. 'What specifically are you driving at, Mr. Brewster?'

'Guns,' Paul said. 'What kind of pistols do you own?'

'Two; a forty-five Army automatic—souvenir from the war—and a .25 Belgian automatic. Look; are you implying I might own the gun which killed Hugo Drexler?'

'I'm not implying anything,' Paul said evenly. 'Is the twenty-five one of a matched pair—a silver and gold overlayed weapon?'

Mallory's manner became chilly. 'I see you've called on Miss Madison,' he said coldly.

'That's right. Is your twenty-five the mate to hers?'

'It is.' Antagonism dripped from the words. 'Look, Mr. Brewster—if you're trying to tie me—or Miss Madison—to Drexler's murder you're wasting your time and mine. I believe we have both proven where we were at six o'clock this morning.'

Paul studied the frank and unmasked rancour in Mallory's face. 'You're an attorney aren't you?' Mallory nodded. His eyes narrowed. Paul went on: 'Then you know we accept nothing until we have the murderer. All we know now is that you and Miss Madison were the last people to see Drexler alive.'

Mallory swung up out of his chair. 'That's ridiculous,' he said. 'We left him around four-thirty yesterday afternoon. He was killed about six the following morning—this morning.'

'In other words you think he probably saw other people after you left him?'

'I say that it's possible.'

'Do you know who he might have seen; are you acquainted with any of his friends or associates?'

'I have no idea who he might have seen,' Mallory said shortly. 'I do know some of the same people he knows but I have no idea which ones might have called on him; all I'm saying is that it's ridiculous to infer that someone who saw him fourteen or fifteen hours before he was killed, is the only person he saw in that length of time.' Mallory measured Paul through his narrowed glance wearing a poorly concealed expression of dislike. 'I *will* say,' he added, 'that the police department is going at this murder in its customary dogmatic and poorly informed way. Now, if you'll excuse me, I'm late for an engagement. If you want me again I'll be either at my office downtown or here at home.'

Paul arose. A second later Mike also got up. He was regarding Mallory stonily. Paul said, 'Mr. Mallory, have you ever owned a .32 calibre pistol?'

'No, I never have. Anything else?'

'Yes; did you recover your stolen car?'

'It was recovered by the police on the beach road.'

'Damaged?'

'They say not. I haven't been down to claim it yet. Apparently some teenage hoodlums stole it for a joy-ride.'

'How did you discover its loss?'

'I am a light sleeper, Mr. Brewster. About three o'clock this morning I heard a car start up in my drive-way, back out very fast, whip around in the street and race away with the tyres squealing. I caught a glimpse of it at the bedroom window. It was my convertible.'

22

Paul nodded, wondering what Golda Madison could ever have seen in this palpable fraud of a man. 'And you reported it,' he said.

'Yes; I got dressed, took the other car to police head-quarters and reported it.'

Paul deliberately swung his head and gazed at the telephone sitting on a small table against the wall. Mike followed his gaze, so did Patrick Mallory. 'Thanks for your time,' Paul said. 'Let's go, Mike.'

They were both conscious of Mallory standing in the open doorway watching them drive away. Mike's lips were pursed, his eyes half-closed and stormy. 'You've got a point,' he said. 'Why didn't he use the phone?'

'For the same reason he gave Golda one of a matched pair of pistols, probably. Mallory's the scheming type. He doesn't do anything on the spur of the moment. He'd stand in his bedroom window and carefully consider the most practical method of recovering the car; the method which would best fit his plans of the moment.'

'And those were . . . ?'

'I don't know, Mike.'

'Why did he give Golda the gun, then?'

'As a reminder—an innuendo. In other words, he had the other one. To make a pair they'd have to be together; symbolism, Mike. He wanted her—the gun was his reminder of that.'

Mike furrowed his forehead in thought.

23

'That's an odd way to remind a woman you're fond of her,' he said, then his face brightened. 'Maybe it was sort of a threat, Paul.'

'Maybe. The thing that sticks in my craw is his alibi. He knew, as soon as you introduced us, that I knew about it, so right away he's contemptuous. "Here's another cop" he thought, "as dumb as the others." That was his attitude from the moment we entered the house.'

'Maybe, but I think that's just his natural behaviour.'

'Maybe, but he's a pretty calm sort of person, Mike. A man not easily rattled. Then why didn't he phone in about the stolen car? He'd surely know the quickest way to recover it would be to let the department know as soon as he possibly could, wouldn't he; getting dressed and driving downtown would waste almost an hour.'

'All right,' Mike said. 'He wanted to establish an alibi. He sure as hell established a good one; if we brought him to trial he'd have half the police force testifying to his whereabouts at the time Drexler got knocked off. You can't beat that.'

'No,' Paul said, 'it'd be hard to beat all right. How would *you* break it? He couldn't have been at Drexler's place when he was murdered; in fact I don't see how he could even be close by when Drexler got it. What could you do with that?'

24

Mike lit a cigarette and stared at its burning end. 'I wouldn't know where to begin,' he said. 'Frankly, in spite of his attitude and a desire I felt back there to pin his ears back, I can't see Mallory as the murderer.' He smoked a moment and gazed at the buildings moving past and said, 'Where are you going now?'

'To the morgue to meet Mr. Drexler.'

The dead-room was cold, sterile and glistening. A morgue attendant slid Drexler's slab out of its cubicle and rolled back the plastic coverlet to show the upper body and face. A small and purplish hole was centred in the body's chest. The attendant pointed.

'Those are the powder burns. The gun that did it wasn't more than inches away for those specks to go through his clothes.'

Paul looked up quickly. 'Who said he was dressed?'

The attendant looked surprised, then flustered, his face flushed bright red. 'Well—wasn't he?' he said.

Paul motioned toward the wall. 'Okay, put him back.' He turned to Mike who was sitting idly on a metal desk swinging one leg. 'No crossed-up identification, Mike?'

'Nope; I checked him out myself, fingerprints, pictures—the works. It's Hugo Drexler without a doubt.'

'What was he wearing when you first saw him?'

'Pyjamas and a maroon silk dressing-gown.

25

I'd say the killer wasn't more than six feet from him when he fired.'

'Okay; let's go back to the squirrel cage.'

They returned to headquarters, turned the car keys in at the desk and rode an elevator to the third floor. In the office Mike dropped down behind his desk and broke open a newspaper lying there. Paul crossed the room and gazed down at the traffic far below. Mike's voice broke the silence.

'Did you see where Gino Kapelli got it last week?'

Paul crossed to the desk and gazed at the newspaper. 'I didn't read the papers at Tahoe. What happened?'

'Someone in a car pulled up beside him out on Fairfax and let him have it through the window. Killed him deader'n a mackeral.'

'Who?'

'I don't know. Been too busy to pick up the gossip.'

'Who's handling it?'

'I think it's Levin and Rasch downstairs. It says here there was a witness. If that's true it shouldn't take long to wrap it up.'

'Someone didn't use their head,' Paul said. 'You can't kill people in broad daylight and not increase your chances of being seen a thousand times over. As far as Kapelli's concerned, I'm surprised he's lived this long.' He flicked through some papers on his own desk then straightened up and started toward the door. 'I'll go see Benton; be back in a little while.'

'Okay,' Mike said without interest and still studying the newspaper. 'Anything particular you want me to do?'

'You might check out the gun registry on Golda and Mallory, then on your way back upstairs stop by the registration desk and see who was on duty when Mallory set up his alibi, and check it out.'

Mike peered from beneath his eyebrows at Paul. 'Anything else,' he said caustically.

Paul met Captain of Detectives Harold Benton in the doorway of his office. Benton was squat, thick and tough. He offered a gruff greeting, shook Paul's hand and said, 'You're looking fit; let's see some smoke on this Drexler case.' He rustled some papers in his hands. 'Anything in particular you want right now? I got a call from the Commissioners' office.'

'No,' Paul said, 'nothing in particular. Just thought I'd let you know I was back.'

'Yeah; well, Mike reported you in this morning before he called you.'

'Did you ever hear of an attorney named Patrick Mallory, or do you know if he's involved with city administration in any way?'

'Nope; never heard of him, and whoever he is he's got no in with city hall, I can tell you that. If you want to rack a lawyer named Mallory—do it. Just be damned sure of your legal grounds first, is all.' Benton scowled; it was like watching a tornado in the making. 'Who the hell is he?'

'A suspect in the Drexler case.'

'Got a make on him?'

'Not yet. Anyway he's got a cinch of an alibi.'

'There's no such thing,' Benton said bluntly. 'I've yet to see an alibi that can't be broken down in court.'

Stung, Paul said, 'Then you've never run across a suspect who was at headquarters when the guy who took his girl away from him got plugged.'

Benton's brows drew lower, his eyes grew stormy. 'Haven't I though,' he said. 'That's not a new dodge.'

'Have you ever seen it broken?'

'Can't recall right off hand. Listen, I've got to go. See you around.'

Paul watched the rolling gait a moment then turned back towards his own office. He said something unpleasant under his breath. Karger's desk was littered with newspaper but Mike was not there. Paul glanced at an opened page and saw the half-page enlargement of Gino Kapelli staring balefully up at him. He picked it up, dropped into his own chair and began to read. Kapelli had been shot in front of the Fidelity Loan Company's offices at 1620, Fairfax Avenue, during the noon-hour.

There was no sense of either loss or elation

in Paul. Kapelli had been a thorn in police flesh for at least six years. Numbers mobster, protection racketeer, hoodlum and three-time loser, he had been high in the city's underworld. Big enough to warrant Treasury Department interest. Paul grimaced. That was one rap Kapelli would beat.

Mike came back wearing an odd expression, half ironic, half amused. He had two sheaves of papers in his hand. Without speaking he tossed both on Paul's desk, crossed to his chair and dropped down, picked up part of the paper and immediately became immersed in it.

'What'd you find?' Paul asked, putting the paper aside slowly.

'The run-down on Drexler to start with. The other's the weapons page with Mallory's name on it.'

Paul looked at the registry sheet first, as he read he said, 'What about Mallory's alibi?'

'I got their names, left word for them to send up reports. Won't be on duty until eleven tonight.'

The registry page showed four pistols under the name of Patrick Mallory. The last entry was for a .32 Colt automatic, number 186400. Pat looked around at Karger with raised eyebrows.

'Did he tell us he had no .32?'

'He did. Look at the date.'

Two years earlier. Paul stared at the page a moment before putting it aside and picking up the rap-sheet of Hugo Drexler. There were four requests for investigations and one notation by the District Attorney's office to the effect that prior to coming to the Coast Drexler had once been indicted for a fraudulent transfer of bonds in New York State. The punishment upon conviction had been six months and full restitution. Paul put the paper down in front of him and lit a cigarette.

'Mike; we'd better get off a teletype to New York.'

'He wasn't shot long distance,' Mike retorted.

'You're sure sarcastic,' Paul said. 'It must be time for your five o'clock feeding.'

Mike rattled the paper, turned a page and said, 'What about Golda.'

'What about her?'

'Why didn't you ask me to bring up her rap-sheet?' Paul looked blank. 'Does she have one?'

'Darned if I know, I didn't look, but if I were you I'd sure consider it.'

Paul swivelled his chair around. For a moment he looked at Mike's profile, then he shrugged before speaking. 'Don't worry, she'll get checked out. There are some things about her that don't fit the part through.'

'Name me one.'

'All right; motive. She was engaged to the guy. Two; the position of that hole in Drexler

30

indicates the guy who shot him was at least as tall as he was—as tall as I am. She's at least six inches shorter.'

Mike laid the paper aside and rummaged in a coat pocket for cigarettes, flipped one out and lit it, put his hands behind his head and squinted through smoke at the ceiling. 'All right,' he said finally in a slightly altered tone of voice. 'Go on—one more.'

'If she'd killed him she'd have rigged up a better alibi than that weak one she has. We can make a fool out of her on that any time we want to.'

Mike took his hands down, removed the cigarette and looked at the ash. 'Okay; just don't overlook the fact that she might be no saint, though.' He inhaled and spiralled past his nose. 'So Mallory's our alternate suspect and I'm here to tell you I hope he doesn't pant out. Getting that bird pinned to the wall will be about as easy as picking flies off a cloud. There's got to be more to it, Paul.'

'There is. Man; we just got it this morning.' He got up with Drexler's record in his hand. 'I'm going down to audit and see if they've come up with anything from the papers you brought in from his apartment.'

There was a cubbyhole office next to Records and Files where a burly man with a withered arm worked at a huge desk. In one corner of the room was a hot-plate with a coffee pot simmering on it. When Paul entered

31

the heavy man peered up at him, blinked and made a remark about the suntan. Paul waved Drexler's record.

'Your turn'll come, Sam. Now, what do you make of this fellow? Mike said he brought some papers on him to you this morning.'

The accountant's twinkling eyes grew sardonic. He stabbed at the papers on his desk with a pencil. 'This much I can tell you, Paul, he was no small-fry. When he made a deal it had six figures in it. Another thing— somewhere around the country he's got a safety-deposit box. He's got to have; these bank books show withdrawals for which I can find absolutely no receipts or records of expenditure. Pretty big figures, too. A guy as foxy as this one wouldn't overlook taking tax deductions on money like this—if he could do it, of course.' The accountant leaned far back and his chair squeaked. 'I'd sum him up as a real smooth operator on a big scale. Not quite beyond the law so far as these records indicate, but I've sent a man out to go over his apartment again; check his bank, credit rating, dig up all he can because this guy fascinates me. Somewhere, somehow, he's a crook. I'll bet you five to one on it. But proving it's going to be hard—real hard.' The accountant's gaze lifted, became sharp and interested. 'You know, Paul; working out the formula of a man's mind can best be done right here.' He tapped the papers. 'You guys with guns—you

32

go find the animal in men. To me this is much more fascinating; it lets me see how their minds work—their brains.'

'This one's brain isn't going to work any more, Sam.'

'Yeah, I know. Mike told me. I'll say this: I don't believe this guy ever got hooked—until he made his last and biggest mistake—then he got out of his element. He was a wizard with figures but apparently couldn't think fast enough to dodge a bullet—it happens.'

'Yeah. Tell me, Sam, did Mike bring in a list of creditors?'

'Yes, there's a partial list here. I don't have it typed up yet, though.' The withered arm sorted through the mass of paper. 'Here.'

'Suppose I keep it until I've run down the leads I can get off it, then bring it back?'

'Sure, only don't forget it; we've got to have the original in our files.'

'I won't and thanks.'

Paul was passing down the long corridor when he met Detective Herbert Rasch coming out of a washroom. Rasch thumped him across the shoulders and showed a dazzling array of gold-tipped teeth in a broad smile. 'Glad to see you back,' he said.

'Glad to be back, Herb. Mike said you're on the Kapelli killing. How's it stacking up?'

'Lousey. Even dead he gives us problems. Got knocked off over on Fairfax, right in the middle of town.'

'Got anything on it yet?'

'We got a witness who saw the guy driving the car. Newspapers've been after Bob and me to get the witness's name. We're cuddling this one like he's a show-girl; he's going to put a torpedo in Death Row for us.'

'Where've you got him?'

'Right here—down in the psycho tank incognito.'

'How about the hoods, any threats against him yet?'

'Well, at first there was some talk around, but lately no.'

'Well, tell Bob hello for me, Herb. See you around.'

Mike was just putting down the telephone when Paul entered. 'Sent the teletype to New York,' he said. 'What did you turn up with?'

Paul sat down and frowned at the tight, snarled scrawl of Hugo Drexler's handwriting. 'A list you brought in; the one with creditors and so forth listed on it.'

'Doorbell work to dig anything out of that,' Mike said. 'Let's take a drive out there; you haven't seen the apartment yet.'

Paul got up, folded the list and pocketed it and stared at Mike. 'I got the impression you were tired, before I went downstairs.'

'Naw; just talked to my wife. We're having cabbage rolls for dinner. I'd rather kill a couple of hours and eat out. Come on, there's a delicatessen on Fairfax that serves the best kosher sandwiches you ever tasted. I ate there this morning when we got the call on Drexler.'

Paul stopped just inside the door. He looked puzzled. 'By the way—just where did Drexler live?'

Mike snagged his hat, dumped it on the back of his head and went around his desk. 'Fairfax. Sixteen-twenty Fairfax. Had an upstairs apartment.' Paul was blocking the doorway without moving. 'Well,' Mike said, 'let's go. What's wrong—you just see a ghost?'

Paul didn't reply. He rode to the street floor beside Mike in the elevator. The building was emptying of people. They pressed and talked and hurried, sweeping the two detectives along with them. Not until they were in a car driving south did he say anything to Mike.

'I saw Herb Rasch. He and Bob Levin have a secret witness to Kapelli's murder.'

Mike snorted. 'Not so secret,' he said, 'I read it in the evening paper.'

'His identity is secret. No one knows his name.'

'Only way he'll stay healthy if Kapelli was rubbed out by gangsters.'

'I know; you haven't talked to Herb or Bob since Drexler's killing have you?'

'No—why? What's the difference.'

'Just wondering,' Paul said. 'No reason I can put my finger on—just curious is all.'

CHAPTER TWO

When Mike parked the sedan in front of the Fidelity Loan Company's darkened office he was whistling to himself and gazing across the street where a black and red sign announced that Sam's Delicatessen served the finest kosher meals in the city. When Paul came around beside him and stopped to gaze up at the darkened windows above the loan company, Mike said, 'Let's eat first.'

Paul shrugged. They crossed the street and entered Sam's place. A thick heavy woman met them with a damp smile. The night was unseasonably warm and a steadily humming air-conditioner worked at keeping the delicatessen five degrees cooler inside.

They ordered and ate. Mike was enjoying his spiced meat rapturously while Paul, glancing over Mike's shoulder and across the street from time to time, appeared absorbed with his own thoughts. When they finished and Mike insisted on picking up the tab, Paul bought a packet of cigarettes he did not need and leaned across the counter where the fat woman was making Mike's change.

'Tell Sam the food is as good as I expected it to be,' he said quietly, 'when he gets back.' He watched her closely, saw the consternation leap into her eyes, the rush of colour under her

36

cheeks, paid for his cigarettes when she made no reply and followed Mike out into the evening.

Mike led the way to Drexler's apartment. He had a key and when he swung the door inward Paul noted the gloominess from drawn blinds and the smell of stale air from closed windows. He crossed the living-room, raised two shades and yanked the cord on a venetian blind. Mike was standing thoughtfully in the middle of the room gazing at the rug.

'He was flat on his back right there,' he said pointing. 'From the way he was lying I think the blast knocked him back a little ways.'

Paul measured the distance with his eye. 'The killer probably knocked on the door,' he said. 'Drexler opened it—maybe he stepped back to let the killer enter when the gun went off.'

'Something like that,' Mike agreed, and looked around the apartment. The furnishings were expensive; the place reeked of money spent lavishly but not with especially good taste.

Paul walked through the rooms, peered into chifferobes, closets, drawers, cupboards, and returned to the living-room where Mike was sitting on a mauve sofa.

'Does the phone work?'

'It did this morning.'

Paul picked it up, dialled headquarters and stood thoughtfully staring out a window at the red casts of sundown sweeping brilliantly out of the west. Almost directly across the way was Sam's Delicatessen; now, a flashing neon sign advertised the store's existence with darting little squirts of light which leapt at you and disappeared in regular intervals.

'Paul Brewster here. Connect me with Rasch and Levin's office, will you.' There was a lull then a brusque voice spoke a name.

'Detective Levin.'

'Hello Bob—Paul Brewster.'

'Hello Paul, Herb told me you were back. What's up?'

'Want me to name your secret witness for you?'

For a moment Levin did not speak. When he did his voice had a reproving sound. 'It's no secret down here, Paul. I guess half a dozen guys know who he is.'

'Well,' Paul said tartly, 'so do I and I've never seen him or talked to anyone but Herb who has—and Herb didn't tell me his name.'

'So?'

'So I think you guys are doing a lousey job of taking care of him.'

'Do you,' Levin said quickly, antagonistically. 'Well, I'd like to see someone get to him—you included.'

Paul remained unruffled. 'Look Bob; I'm on the Drexler case. Mike and I just had dinner at a delicatessen on Fairfax. The woman running the place has a face like a book—one look and

38

you know her secret. You and Herb think your star witness can't be gotten to, but all anyone has to do is throw the fear of God into Mrs. Sam and I'll give you any odds you want that Sam won't stand up for you in court.' When Levin's breathing came over the telephone, but no other sound, Paul went on. 'Suppose they knocked her off, Bob? If the cops get close they will—providing they find out who she is and where her husband is—which wouldn't be hard. What would that do to your witness?'

'I thought of that,' Levin said. 'Suppose we put cops around her; that'd be like telling the world, Paul.' Levin paused. 'Look; we've gone over this pretty well. If we bring her in for protective custody like we did with Sam— Kapelli's killers'll know in a couple of hours who we've got.'

'And?'

'Simple. They'll go to work on the relatives. Any way you look at it the best thing is to let her pass the word Sam's out of town for a few days. Another thing, one of us contacts her regularly. No one's been around to enquire about Sam except the family, so the hoods don't know Sam's our finger yet.'

'But you're a long way from trial, Bob. Between now and then someone's likely to tumble.'

Levin sounded exasperated. 'Maybe, Paul, we've turned the thing over until it's worn thin.

At first there was some interest in the underworld, but lately our pipelines indicate the interest has quieted down.'

'You mean you believe that some hood—with the lethal chamber staring him in the face—isn't interested enough in his own welfare to try and find out who is going to put him in Death Row? Bob; you're kidding yourself. If things're quiet it's because the murderer knows he's got a couple of months to go before he'll be picked up.'

'He hasn't got two days,' Bob Levin said. 'All we need is to know where he's hiding; we know who he is. We're waiting out the stoolies who'll find out where he is, that's all, then we arrest him and that's that.'

'You're a dreamer,' Paul said. 'With only one witness to put him away—even after you arrest him—he'll have friends who'll go to work on Sam's family. But okay; it's your baby, Bob.' He hung up and leaned on the wall. Mike smoked and waited for him to speak, when he didn't Mike spoke.

'So their witness is the guy from the delicatessen.'

'Yeah. Mike, I've got a feeling there's a link here somewhere. Gino Kapelli got killed two weeks ago under Drexler's window. What could that mean?'

'A coincidence,' Mike said.

'Maybe, but I've got a feeling we're about to stumble on to something else. Let's go back downtown.'

When they put the car away Paul moved briskly across the pavement and through the lobby. Waiting for the elevator, he gazed at Mike with narrowed eyes and just when Mike was going to speak the elevator arrived. They both got in and rode to the third floor. When Paul opened the door to his office, Herb Rasch and Bob Levin looked up at them from their desks. 'Thought you birds were going to make a night of it,' Rasch said, vacating Mike's chair.

Paul sat down, tilted his chair back against the wall and waited. But Levin only grunted. Mike was scowling at the visitors and when the silence had stretched thin he said, 'Your man got killed at sixteen-twenty-two Fairfax and our man had an apartment at sixteen-twenty.'

'So?' Levin said. 'After we talked I ran a make on your man. What connection would there be between a hood like Kapelli and an operator like this Drexler—tell me that, will you?'

'Could be anything,' Paul said. 'Drexler was a shady character. You must have figured that from his rap-sheet, Bob.'

'All right; but worlds apart from Kapelli. Drexler steered clear of violence and Kapelli steered clear of brains—now where's the connection?'

'What's Sam's last name?'

'Pearlman. Sam Pearlman. What about it?'

'And you told me the underworld isn't

worried about your secret witness. That no one's done much threatening for the past few days.'

'That's right,' Herb Rasch said. 'We've kept taps out. For a while there was a rumble. It died away and now no one seems to care about the witness any more.'

'And you guys think maybe the murderer was an out of town gun, or he's faded.'

'We know who he is,' Levin said. 'We got everything but him.'

Paul shook his head. 'That's not the point,' he said.

'The hell it isn't,' Levin said. 'In a killing what counts is the killer.' His lower lip was thrust out. 'What else do you want; motive? A guy like Kapelli's a walking motive for half the city to plug him. What else you want?'

Paul grinned into the truculent face, lit a cigarette and offered the pack. When the others were smoking he tossed the cigarettes on his desk and said, 'I want a motive for several things. Kapelli's yours; I don't care about him except indirectly.'

'Seems to me you're pretty interested,' Levin said tartly, 'for a disinterested guy.'

'Look, Bob. Let's suppose someone read in the papers you have a witness to the Kapelli killing. That was two weeks ago, wasn't it?'

'Yes.'

'How long did it take Pearlman to get up guts enough to come in and say he'd witnessed

42

the killing?'

'A week after it happened.'

'That answers one thing for me,' Paul said, then he went on without explaining. 'So. Hugo Drexler lived upstairs from where Kapelli got it . . .'

'My God,' Herb Rasch said abruptly. 'Sure. Bob that figures. Kapelli's killer heard about our witness—read about it and somehow got the notion this Drexler was it, so he shot him.'

Bob Levin's undershot lip receded a little. He was looking at Paul Brewster without blinking. Finally he said, 'Is that what's in your mind?'

Paul countered with a question of his own. 'Does it figure?'

Levin looked at Mike with a slow nod. 'It could figure,' he said. 'Well—now we want him for one definite murder and suspicion of another one.'

Paul crushed his cigarette and creased his forehead. 'But Mike and I don't want your killer especially, boys. You see, we've got another notion about the Drexler case.'

Mike was looking at Paul with a blank face. Bob Levin was silent, wearing an expression of anticipatory respect. 'Go on,' he said.

'We've got a man in the Drexler case who thinks cops are dumb clods. He's got a fool-proof alibi for the time Drexler got knocked off. He was right here at headquarters reporting a car theft.'

43

'That's airtight,' Rasch said.

'It's too good,' Paul replied. 'It's so good it smells preconceived to me. Now let's assume this man knew Drexler was going to get it.'

'Is he a hood?' Levin asked.

Paul shrugged. 'By trade he's a lawyer. A pretty successful one from appearances, but we'll know more about that after we've checked him out. Now the idea I've got is this: Our man wanted Drexler killed—we know that, or are pretty sure of it anyway.'

'Why?'

'A woman,' Mike said. 'A real picture of a woman.'

Levin nodded and returned his glance to Paul. 'So this guy wanted Drexler knocked off over a woman—go on.'

'There was no absolutely safe way he could kill Drexler, you see, and being a lawyer he'd know about alibis. He'd know the only way for a murderer to be absolutely safe would be to have the killing done in such a way that he couldn't be connected to it. He's that type; very shrewd, highly educated—a lawyer.'

'So he hired the job done,' Rasch said.

Paul shook his head. 'Better than that, Herb. He read about your secret witness and knew the underworld would do anything to get to him. It was a natural situation for him. Kapelli got it right outside the apartment of his worst enemy. He simply saw to it that the word was passed around the underworld that

44

this enemy of his—this Hugo Drexler—was the witness. The rest was bound to happen. A hood called on Drexler—who was unsuspecting. When Drexler opened the door . . .' Paul made the motion of a man pulling a trigger.

For some seconds no one spoke, then Levin asked how Paul had come to his conclusions?

'Mike and I went to see this man this morning. His name's Patrick Mallory. We were standing less than ten feet from a telephone when Mallory told us he got *dressed* and *drove* to headquarters to report the car theft. Look; here's a successful attorney, calm as they come, knowing all the ropes about how the department works and that speed is the secret of catching car thieves—and he deliberately kills an hour by driving to headquarters instead of phoning about his stolen car. It's as phoney a yarn as I've ever heard but it established him with the perfect alibi. 'You know what I think? I think this is the first case in the department's history where the perfect alibi is going to prove too perfect—so perfect it will break itself.'

Mike was nodding his head up and down. When Paul stopped talking he said, 'You guys drag the killer in and we'll sweat the story out of him. Both cases will be closed in less than a week. That's what Cap Benton likes.'

Rasch squirmed uncomfortably in his chair and looked at Levin, who said, 'It won't be that simple, Mike. The killer disappeared. We thought we had a lead on him until this morning. In fact we were going to close in when one of our informers called in that he'd flown.'

'This morning?' Paul said. Levin nodded and Paul let his chair down off the wall, stood up, thrust fisted hands deep into his trouser pockets and went over to stare down out of the window.

Mike, Herb Rasch and Bob Levin talked desultorily for several moments, then grew silent. They eyed Paul's back and Levin got up, stretched and groped for another cigarette. 'I wish we could have known sooner, Paul.'

'How could you? We didn't have a corpse until this morning.' Paul turned back into the room.

Levin smoked. 'We've been expecting Benton to explode in our faces ever since Kapelli got it,' he said. 'I'm getting so's I cringe when I see him in the corridor.'

Paul went back to his chair and dropped down. 'He couldn't do any better,' he said. 'You can't pick suspects out of thin air, but I've an idea how you can get your man and maybe we can find out if Mallory is implicated.'

'How?'

'Tell the reporters Drexler was your witness.'

'Huh?'

'Tell them Hugo Drexler was your secret

witness—that the underworld must have found it out and killed him. When that story hits the streets your killer might come out of hiding— at any rate he'll think you have nothing but a suspicion rap to pick him up on, and any smart hood knows a suspicion rap with nothing concrete behind it is useless to us.'

'How would that help us?' Mike asked.

'Easy,' Paul replied. 'As soon as the hood gets back into circulation he's arrested, confronted with Sam Pearlman who identifies him, and if he's smart he'll try to make a deal with the D.A's office and save his neck by putting the finger on whoever told him Drexler was the secret witness. If it was Mallory we can tie him in as an accessory to murder—if it wasn't Mallory, we'll still have an accessory.'

'Wait a minute,' Bob Levin said. 'There's a flaw to this. This Mallory—or whoever tipped the killer off about Drexler—knows darned well Drexler *didn't* witness Kapelli's murder. The killer himself wouldn't know it, but the other guy would, Paul.'

'So he knows,' Paul retorted. 'Just as long as the *killer* doesn't know there's a pretty good chance he'll come out of hiding.'

Mike looked disappointedly at the floor. 'But he'll get to the killer, warn him.'

Paul shook his head. 'I'm betting he won't because he's far too smart to get directly implicated in a murder. My notion is that he spread the tale that Drexler was the man

47

without leaving any trail back to him that would indicate he started the story. There won't be any way to link him with to the actual murder.'

Herb Rasch was filling a pipe from a scuffed pouch. 'And I thought we had a tough case *before* Pearlman came in,' he said.

Bob Levin's forehead was crinkled. 'The toughest part no one's mentioned yet. Look; suppose Paul's theorising is all wrong. Suppose we don't nail a killer and he doesn't pin anything on this Mallory. Do you guys know what the newspapers'll do to us? They're already hostile over our refusal to name our secret witness—if we come out now and name Drexler, and they find out later he wasn't the witness—that we were using them to spread a lie for us—man—I hate to think what they'll print.'

'The answer to that,' Paul said, 'depends on how many people know who Pearlman is.' He was looking at Levin.

'The Commissioner knows,' Levin said, 'and Cap Benton. Aside from them only the men in this room and one jailer knows Pearlman's name and why he's in protective custody.'

'How about the killer?'

Levin removed an envelope from his pocket, opened it and shook out a typewritten page with a small picture of a man's face stapled in the upper corner. He held it out for Paul to take.

48

'Anthony Clampetti. Four time loser out on parole. Been booked for everything in the book but murder.'

Paul passed the sheet to Mike Karger. 'Better get us one,' he said, 'the next time you're downstairs.' He got up again and stretched. 'You'd better brief Cap Benton, Bob. He'll want to know there's a possible tie-in between the two murders. See you fellows tomorrow.'

Mike returned the paper on Anthony Clampetti and closed the door behind Levin and Rasch. Paul had taken his chair over by the window and was sitting there, feet cocked up, a tendril of cigarette smoke winding upwards past his partially closed eyes. Mike picked up his hat, looked at Brewster's back a moment, then said good night. Paul answered without turning around and Mike left the office.

Beyond the window myriad lights spanked the underneath of a giant width of dark shadow which was night. The city's ceaseless and quiet growl rose straight up. As far as the eye could see, and farther, were patterns of streets fanning out, flanked by lights, some moving, some still. The telephone rang. Paul turned, looked at it, gazed at his wristwatch, arose and crossed to the desk.

'Brewster—homicide.'

'This is Golda Madison, Mr. Brewster.'

He glanced at his watch again and frowned.

'Good evening.'

'I've been thinking about Hugo ever since you left this morning.'

'Come up with anything helpful?'

'No; I thought you might have an idea, though.'

'Afraid not,' he lied blandly.

'Hugo *was* the kind of a man who could make deadly enemies,' she said.

'You didn't think so this morning, Miss Madison.'

For a moment she said nothing. '. . . I don't suppose the average person looks at their acquaintances from the viewpoint of a policeman, Mr. Brewster. It requires certain adjustments. Since this morning I've been remembering things about Hugo; things which might be considered—well—cold and unpleasant by others.'

He turned slightly, gazed out the window, perched on the edge of the desk and watched deep night settle thicker, gathering depth and perspective as it muffled the tumult far below in the cement canyons. 'Suppose I drop by in an hour or so and talk about him with you.

Another pause, then: 'Tonight?'

'Yes.'

'Well; all right.' There was reluctance and doubt in her tone. 'All right, Mr. Brewster.'

He hung up and sat there looking down at the telephone. Why had she called? What was really on her mind? To pump him, find out if the police were making headway? Possibly; was it just curiosity? Again—possibly. He picked up his hat, held it without putting it on. Golda and Mallory . . . He was afraid of Mallory. A murderer smart enough to engineer a killing by remote control was smart enough to avoid implication. To top that, Mallory was an attorney, a successful one, too, if appearances meant anything. *If* Mallory had planned Drexler's murder the way Paul had it deduced, the weakest link in his chain of circumstantial evidence was that Mallory wouldn't believe what the papers said about Drexler actually being the secret witness, and if that was true, Mallory would waste no time passing the word the newspaper story was a hoax and for the killer to remain in hiding. Additionally, Attorney Mallory knew how the police operated; probably had informants of his own within the department. Paul went as far as the door before donning his hat. He would pass the word in the morning that a lawyer named Mallory was not, under any circumstances, to be told anything at all about the Kapelli or Drexler murder cases.

On the drive to Golda Madison's several ideas went through his mind. A check of the records would show which underworld characters had been clients of Mallory's. A few arrests ought to clear up doubts about whether his theory about Mallory passing the word which got Drexler killed was correct or incorrect. There was bound to be some hoodlum who would know the answer to that. From there—*if* he got the information he hoped for—some careful and tactful sleuthing ought to turn up at least enough evidence to support his theory; possibly even enough to warrant bringing Mallory in for questioning. The biggest single factor was that regardless of what Paul turned up, Mallory could not be arraigned for murder, and that rankled more than anything else.

Just before he parked and looked up at the long, wide planes of orange light coming from Golda Madison's apartment, he had another idea. There might be a way to frighten Mallory badly enough to make him come to the police of his own accord. If there was—*if* he could be put upon the defensive—Paul would have an even chance of bringing him to justice. He got out of the car and explored the idea: If Mallory saw through his ruse to put the actual murderer off guard and let it leak down into the underworld that Drexler wasn't the witness, Paul could retaliate by letting it slip to the shadowy men who sold information to the department that someone was out to kill Mallory for supplying false information—for getting a personal enemy killed and jeopardising a killer's life by trickery. Gangsters were notorious for their sensitivity about being out-smarted. When word spread that one of them at least had been deliberately used by an attorney named Mallory, underworld derision would do the rest.

Paul lit a cigarette, flipped the match into the gutter and gazed at the lighted windows. As he watched a shadow moved past. He smoked and watched and thought she would be the ideal medium to reach Mallory through. When the cigarette was finished he flipped it after the match and started toward the building.

Golda met him at the door. Her hair shone with dark light and her smile was tentatively warm, as though she wasn't certain of her ground. 'Can I get you a high-ball?'

He moved to the chair she indicated, put his hat aside and nodded.

'That would be wonderful; I'm a little tired tonight.'

When she returned she had two glasses. The sound of ice was pleasant. He took his drink with a nod and watched her cross to a sofa and sit down. Her glance was enquiringly direct and level.

'The shock all gone?' he asked.

She put the glass on an end-table. 'I suppose it'll take time,' she said coolly. 'Not having him call, drop by . . .' She swung her head toward him. 'You made it plain enough this morning that you didn't think I cared very much for him.'

'You said you weren't sure you'd marry him.'

'I know, but evidently your knowledge of people doesn't include much experience with women. I'm not a child any more; there was no intense and possessive passion, Mr. Brewster.'

He finished the drink and toyed with the glass, looked down into it. Female abstractions were not, it was very true, in his line. He switched the subject.

'I called on Mr. Mallory this morning. He didn't like the idea of my visit here earlier.'

'Yes, I know, he called me. He is a high-strung person, Mr. Brewster. I know he can be antagonistic at times but I think when you know him better you'll like him.'

Paul's face was expressionless. 'Drexler was also antagonistic at times, I assumed from your conversation this evening.'

She leaned back and gazed past him. 'Hugo was very different from Pat. It's very hard to explain. He had a knack of writing the most immaturely insulting things to people, but fundamentally he wasn't mean. Actually, I think he felt insecure, possibly inferior, and I do know that once he sent Pat one of those letters and when Pat went over to see him about it Hugo was apologetic.'

'You're making him sound like a coward.'

'Well; perhaps he was, but if he was a coward it was only in the physical sense, Mr. Brewster. I never knew a man who would take calculated risks like Hugo Drexler.'

'Give me an example.'

'In financial matters,' she said, and her voice dwindled into silence while they exchanged a long look. Paul was remembering something she had said that morning; something about being unfamiliar with Drexler's business activities. He could tell from her expression she was also remembering that.

'Was he your financial adviser, Miss Madison?'

'Oh no; Pat Mallory's been that for years. Hugo resented it, he told me he did. Pat still advises me in financial matters.'

'Then what did you mean about Drexler?'

She shrugged. 'Little things. Nothing of importance really. Comments he dropped from time to time. After all, you can't be close to someone and not pick up things you know.'

'Yes, I know,' he said distinctly. 'From these little things he let drop you built up some idea of his activities.'

'Well; but not the way you meant this morning. Only that Hugo considered certain stocks worthwhile, others poor risks—things like that.' She smiled at him. 'This morning you meant his secret life—something like that.'

'Did he have a secret life?'

The smile died. 'That was a term of speech—an expression; of course Hugo had no secret life.' She drew forward on the cushions. 'Mr. Brewster, don't be dogmatic.'

It was his turn to smile. There was some genuine humour in it but not very much. 'I'm a policeman; a man's been murdered . . .'

'But it's after working hours.' She inclined her lovely head toward the empty highball glass. 'You wouldn't do that while you were working, would you?'

He also looked at the glass. 'No,' he said slowly, 'not habitually, but a policeman with a problem isn't much different from anyone else with something on his mind; he thinks about it pretty steadily—at least until he's satisfied that he'd work it out.'

'Even on a beautiful summer night?'

'Even on a beautiful summer night, and with a lovely woman to look at, Miss Madison.' He thought it was time to pick up his hat and leave but made no move to arise. 'By the way, will you show me that Indian ruin one of these days?'

The twinkle returned to her eyes. 'Certainly; in fact I had an idea that might come up in our conversation this evening.'

He felt his face redden and that time he did get up, pick up his hat and look down at her. He wanted to make a crisp, short answer, but knew she wouldn't believe him, so he said, 'Were you sure it would?'

'No; not until just now, Mr. Brewster.' She stood up. 'Now I understand that the reason it came up was simply because you're a policeman on a case.'

He went to the door, turned the knob and said, 'Tomorrow forenoon?'

'Afternoon would be better,' she said.

He nodded, thanked her and left. Down in the patio he stopped to light a cigarette, gaze up at the two tall, lighted windows and shake his head slightly. Behind that beautiful exterior was more: a knowledge of men, of course. A woman as heady as Golda Madison would know about men, but there was something else he sought to identify and could not. Shrewdness; cleverness . . . He went out to the car, got in and touched the starter.

He lay for a long time in the dark of his bedroom trying to evaluate Golda Madison. So far as Mallory was concerned, he had small doubt about his appraisal. Golda Madison was the unknown quotient—and, of course, everything he did or said around her went right back to Mallory—and yet, somehow, Paul had the impression she cared no more for Mallory than she had for Drexler. Was it cold-bloodedness, or had *she* a hand in the murder; wasn't it possible *both* she and Mallory had? He answered that affirmatively to himself and slept on it, awakened with it still uppermost in his mind and when he got to headquarters it was still there.

Mike came in fresh and shiny looking, all except up around the eyes. He squatted on his chair and scowled. 'Paul—'

'Hold it a minute,' Paul said. 'I've got something on my mind, Mike.'

'You should have,' Mike interrupted dourly.

57

'If this theorising of yours lays an egg, brother . . .'

'I want to bug Golda Madison's telephone.'

Mike didn't move. 'You're walking barefoot over razor-blades,' he said. 'Look; let's just play it smart for a day or two. Have you seen the papers—how they played up that dead witness angle? Went for it hook, line and sinker.' Mike took a crushed tabloid from a coat pocket and held it out. 'Look,' he said.

Paul roused himself and read. The story was bannered across the front page. Inside, his heart lurched; if this didn't work out he'd have to resign. Every reporter, editor and newspaper publisher in the State would dishonour him, not to mention the politicaIly-appointed Police Commissioner who lived on newspaper backing and whose party was facing some rugged competition in the forthcoming primary elections which were not many weeks off.

Mike was smiling. 'They made it so plausible,' he said, 'I could believe it myself if I didn't know it was a pack of lies.'

Paul winced. 'It's good coverage all right,' he said without enthusiasm.

'Good? It's just what we wanted. But from here on we've got to make it better.'

'That's why I want the Madison line tapped. I went out there and had a highball with her last night,' Paul said pushing aside the newspaper. 'It'll have to be strictly an unofficial tap, Mike.'

'I know that.'

'What I had in mind was for you to slip in, make the tap and plant the earphone.'

'Me?' Karger said loudly. 'Why me? It's your idea. Besides, you know what'd happen if we got caught, don't you?'

'Yes, I know.' Paul drew a finger across his throat.

'Anyway, how could it be worked?'

'I'm taking Miss Madison up to the Indian ruin where Drexler tumbled off the wall this afternoon. That'll get her miles away from the apartment.'

'Sure, but how about the maid? She's no dummy, Paul.'

'Cut it out, Mike. You know all the diversion angles.'

'Okay, okay; I can get her out of the house for the length of time required for the job— but why should I? Give me a good reason, will you?'

'I'm pretty sure she's relaying everything we do to Mallory. I want to make sure. If we can tap a conversation between them it'd help to beat hell, wouldn't it?'

'If they said something incriminating,' Mike agreed, 'sure, but it wouldn't be admissible in court.'

'We wouldn't present it in court. All we want is a sound lead tying one or the other, or both, to Drexler's killing. After that we know

59

what we're trying to prove.'

'Wouldn't it be better to bug Mallory's line?'

Paul got up and walked around his desk, perched on the edge of it shaking his head. 'Maybe later. Maybe after we've definitely linked him with the crime, but right now I want to know whether Golda's tied in or not.'

'Sure,' Mike said softly, gazing at Paul. 'Sure that's all you want. Want me to tell you why; because you've got stardust in your eyes, Paul. You don't *want* this beauty involved in a murder. Look; Golda Madison and Marilyn Monroe could pull a milkwagon through town naked and you know what I'd be thinking while I was watching; how I'm going to make the next car payment.' Paul retrieved the paper folded it meticulously and put in on his own desk. 'If Golda tumbles or if Mallory gets an idea we've bugged her telephone and squawks to the D.A., I hope the thought of her gorgeous grey eyes keeps you warm next winter while you're out job hunting.'

'Then come up with something else,' Paul said shortly.

'I can't; not from *her* angle anyway. All I want out of this is a murderer and a case-folder marked "Closed". I don't want to prove somebody *isn't* guilty—I want to prove somebody *is* guilty.'

'You won't do it, then?'

Mike looked resigned. 'I didn't say that. I just wanted you to know that I know how your mind works. Sure I'll do it. If you weren't going out with her this afternoon I'd let you do it—but that's out so I'm elected. But I want you to know what I think of it, too.'

'Mike—'

'Never mind that stuff. I got an attic full of platitudes. Just what exactly do you think she's going to say—or he's going to say—that'll help us?'

'Maybe some mention of that .32 registered to him two years ago. By the way; anything from Lab on the slug they dug out of his wall?'

Mike shook his head. 'Not that I know,' he said, 'but I can find out in a few minutes. Look, Paul, Mallory's not going to slip up on anything as obvious as the murder gun—you know that.'

'All I know is that he said he didn't or hadn't owned a .32 and the registry shows that he once did. For lack of something better I'm hanging on to that like grim death. I'm hoping bugging her line will turn up something better.' He got off the desk and moved toward the door.

'Where you off to?'

'Downstairs. I want to talk to Rasch and Levin.'

Bob Levin was in but Herb Rasch was not. Levin lit a cigarette when Paul entered and spat tobacco off the tip of his tongue while he was nodding. His expression was austere.

'Have you seen the papers this morning?'

61

Paul nodded and Levin slumped over his desk. 'I got a horrible feeling we're going to wind up holding a sack full of something not very pleasant, Paul.'

'I won't deny the risk,' Paul said, 'but it's a calculated one, Bob. Put yourself in Mallory's boots. Suppose you read about Drexler actually being the witness —you'd be surprised to say the least.'

'Yeah, and ten minutes later I'd bust out laughing at the stupid police department, too, for making his murder even safer for me.'

'And you'd go right on laughing until you got an anonymous phone call that someone was mad as hell at you for engineering Drexler's killing for purely personal reasons— and the angry gunman was out for revenge for being used like that. Then you'd quit laughing in a big hurry, wouldn't you? *Then* you'd begin sweating, Bob.'

Levin contemplated the hairs on the back of his hand for a moment, then he looked up and his expression had cleared a little. 'So he'll sweat. Maybe it'll scare hell out of him. Does he come to the police for protection?'

'That is exactly what I'm praying will happen. You can see for yourself if he does come around, we'll know we've hit the nail on the head; that he was threatened.'

'Knowing that, we can be fairly certain he engineered this Drexler guy's rub-out—right?'

'Right.'

'So—have you spread the story about Mallory to the informers yet?'

'Not yet. I'll do it today sometime.'

Levin's scowl returned. 'Don't put if off, Paul, something might happen to queer us—I don't know what but I got very little faith in theories at their best and since our talk last night I got worms crawling under my skin. Sometimes I think I was crazy to go along with you on this—other times I think it's got the makings of a real clever piece of work.' Levin ran blunt fingers through crinkly hair. 'I don't know—can't make up my mind—but play it close to your chest, Paul. It isn't only your neck, it's all the other necks too, including mine, remember.' He puckered up his eyes, leaned far back in his chair and studied Paul Brewster. 'It's a gamble—a long, long gamble.'

'How else could we nab a man like Mallory? He's an attorney, he's intelligent, he's got an air-tight alibi, he's wealthy; the type of criminal you run across once in your police career and you don't expect to nail him when you run across him. Well; if he's our man I'm going to nail him to the wall. He thinks cops are dumb—I want to show him *all* of them aren't dumb.'

Levin's appraisal grew sardonic. 'Paul,' he said crisply. 'You aren't making this a personal matter are you? Listen; you know better than to do that. You know the cop who bends theories to fit a crime is trying to send one

63

man away—he's not trying to solve a crime.'

'It isn't that, Bob. I want the murderer and I want him on the up and up and when I get him I know it isn't going to be Mallory. But I also want to get Mallory and get him good *if* he's mixed up—but only if he is.'

'Okay; just warning you. Is there anything in particular you want me and Herb to do?'

'Yes; find Kapelli's killer.'

Levin spread his hands on the desk. 'We're trying,' he said.

'No, not like you should. Stir up your stoolies, put out a private dragnet, offer funds for information—really go after it, Bob. Dig into the slime until wherever he's hiding someone'll find him and tip you off.'

'Okay—so we'll dig.'

Paul leaned on the door a moment before speaking. 'We've got to snag this murderer the second he shows, Bob, because sure as the devil someone's going to figure things out for him: Kapelli was killed two weeks before Drexler was—someone's going to tell him Drexler *must* have identified him for us before he got killed.'

Paul left the office after Levin glanced up at him in a strange way and groaned aloud. He was grinning to himself. After a little searching Levin would remember that, even if the killer knew he had been identified, the police could produce no living witness and all the circumstantial evidence under the sun

64

wouldn't insure the death penalty. But it was enough to arouse Levin, stir him up and keep him stirred up.

Mike wasn't in their office. Paul crossed to the window and stood there watching the traffic. He was aware of the building's hum and activity, of the gently spreading sheen of morning warmth beyond the window, and he was also aware that a man's future and career were hanging by one little word—IF. If Mallory was implicated to the extent Paul believed him to be; if Mike could safely tap Golda Madison's telephone; if Golda said anything incriminating over it; if Kapelli's murderer could be located within the next eighteen hours; if—

'Paul?'

Mike was closing the door and his expression was down at the mouth.

'That .32 Colt automatic was an incorrect entry. They called while you were out and I went down to confirm it. When the page was typed that Colt automatic was supposed to be listed to a guy named Mulloy —the name right under Mallory, see?'

'I see. Well; that answers what you were wondering, doesn't it? It also lets Mallory off the only hook we had him on, too.'

Mike went to his desk and sat down. 'I stopped by the telephone room—no answer on the inquiry about Drexler yet. I'll re-check later.' He looked at his wristwatch. 'What time're you leaving for the ruin?'

'After lunch.' The telephone rang, he scooped it up and spoke his name. 'Brewster—homicide.'

'Golda Madison, Mr. Brewster.'

'Well; good morning.'

'Good morning. Mr. Brewster; would you mind terribly if Pat Mallory went with us today? He called a short time ago you see, and when I said we were going out there . . .'

'No, I wouldn't mind at all.'

He hung up and gazed at Mike who was carefully assembling some wires and dark, bakelite objects upon his desk with fastidious attention to detail.

'That was Miss Madison, Mike. Patrick Mallory wants to go to the ruin with us this afternoon.'

'Fine,' Mike replied without looking up. 'Maybe he wants to shove you off a wall, too.' He worked a moment longer then leaned back and traced out the wiring pattern with his eyes, nodded in satisfaction and looked up. 'Why? Did she say why?'

'Only that she'd told him about us going out there and he wanted to go along.'

'It'll cramp your style a little,' Mike grunted, 'having her boy friend along.'

A man rolled his fist over the office door then entered before either detective said anything, handed Paul a long and perforated sheet of paper and hurried out, all without

66

speaking. Paul read slowly for a moment, then flicked the paper with a finger. 'Drexler's record from New York.' The telephone interrupted him. Mike picked it up spoke his name, grunted and held it out.

'Benton.'

'Yes, Captain.'

'Come up to my office for a moment, Paul.'

He hung up, handed the teletype to Mike and walked out of the office and up the hall, into Benton's reception room and past the secretary who wore her hair swept up and piled on top of her head, which made an open fretwork of a face horsy unattractive. She buzzed the inner office as Paul moved past.

Benton had a man sitting beside his desk when Paul entered, he managed an introduction without arising. 'This is Mr. Corte of the District Attorney's office, Paul. Pull up a chair.'

Paul drew up and sat down with a cold feeling in his stomach. Corte was well dressed and bright appearance. Benton picked up some papers from a pile on his desk and discourteously began reading them as he spoke.

'Mr. Corte's got something he thought might interest us—something from the immigration people, Paul. You explain, Mr. Corte.'

The D.A's man was not unaware of Captain Benton's rudeness; his reaction was mirrored in a cold look when he swung his chair a little to face Paul. 'An automobile belonging to an attorney named Patrick Mallory was stolen a few nights back according to police files downstairs, Mr. Brewster. It was impounded, gone over, then released upon Mallory's proof of ownership. Are you familiar with the incident?'

Paul held out his cigarette packet, got a refusal and lit one for himself. 'I'm familiar with the incident all right,' he said, 'in fact I'm working on a case involving the car's owner.'

'Fine. Last night the port immigration authorities picked up a suspected illegal entrant who had eight hundred dollars in cash on his person. When he was questioned his man said he'd been paid one thousand dollars cash to steal Mallory's car, drive it up the coast highway and abandon it. When this information was sent to our office the District Attorney asked me to verify it through your records, which brought me up here to Captain Benton—there was a notation on the auto theft sheet that Patrick Mallory was involved in a homicide investigation.'

Paul was sitting on the edge of his chair. He said, 'Yes, Mallory's involved in a case we're trying to break, Mr. Corte, and I believe you've just given us the break we need. I haven't checked out the prints on Mallory's car yet—the murder only happened yesterday morning—but I'm going to do it as soon as I leave

68

here, then, if they tally with this immigration bureau prisoner, I think we can get somewhere.'

'You ought to be able to,' Corte said. 'I'm curious about why someone would pay this man a thousand dollars in cash to steal Mallory's car, drive it up the highway and ditch it.' Corte stood up, he had thawed considerably. 'If anything comes of this I'd sure appreciate it if you'd keep our office informed.' He extended his hand and Paul shook it heartily. 'One thing, Mr. Brewster— Immigration told me they would deport this man no later than day after tomorrow . . .'

'I'll get around to him before that, and after I do I'll see that you're kept posted.'

Corte left and Captain Benton peered from beneath his brows at Paul. 'Mallory do it?' he asked.

'I hope so,' Paul said. 'I hope he did it a thousand dollars worth.'

CHAPTER THREE

It took time to check the fingerprint on Mallory's car because, while there were prints, a profusion of them scattered recklessly or ignorantly throughout the interior of the car, local files could not match them. They were wired to Washington as a matter of police routine but Paul thought a better idea would be for someone from the Lab to take imprints from the man being held by Immigration. Accordingly a technician was sent out.

Paul then returned to the office and made four telephone calls to underworld informants. He did not identify himself beyond saying he knew for a fact that the killer of Hugo Drexler had murdered an innocent man and that whoever had put him up to it had done so in order to have Drexler killed at no cost.

Mike listened with a deep set of vertical lines creasing his forehead between the eyes. When Paul finished he asked for an explanation. Paul briefed him on what the District Attorney's office had discovered. 'I think it's the missing link on Mallory,' he said in conclusion. 'It's probably the reason he was at headquarters reporting a car theft. What I hope turns up is that this illegal entrant can identify Mallory as the man who gave him the thousand dollars.'

'That'll clinch it,' Mike said, face clearing.

'No,' Paul said. 'This one is a puzzler, Mike. No sooner do you think of an angle than you have to consider what Mallory's going to think, and try to out-guess him.'

'What're you talking about?'

'Look; there's no law that says a man can't hire someone to drive his car out of town and ditch it.'

'There's a law against giving the police

70

department false information—how about the city ordinances against creating a nuisance by causing us to make an investigation for no cause?'

'Misdemeanours, Mike. He'd be fined maybe fifty dollars, that's all.'

'Nevertheless it'd be enough to haul him in on.'

'Sure, but when we bring him in—if we do— let's make blessed sure it's on better grounds than a misdemeanour. In the first place he'd be out on habeas corpus before we got him booked. In the second place we don't want him to know we're after him.' Paul glanced at his watch. 'I'd better get going,' he said. 'You got the bugging idea worked out?'

'Yes.'

The door burst inward and Captain Benton filled the opening. He eyed Paul critically before he spoke, then said, 'I got a report saying this Drexler and the Kapelli killing might have a tie-in. That right?'

'I don't know whether it's right or not, but it's sure possible. Mike and I'm working with Herb Rasch and Bob Levin against the possibility there may be a connection.'

'Who was this Drexler; what's his connection with Kapelli?'

'I don't think there was a direct connection, Cap, but it's very likely the man who killed one killed the other.'

Benton nodded in silent thought for a

moment then he looked up sharply. 'Are you making headway—I mean, did that Corte fellow's information pay off?'

'We're making headway, yes, but so far I haven't been able to verify much that Corte said.'

'Well dammit, don't waste time. And here's something else you can chew on: The Commissioner was in to see me yesterday. Primary election time isn't far off and he wants something spectacular to toss at the voters. If this Drexler-Kapelli business shapes up into a dual murder, and you can break it down within the next few days, it'll be about what he wants. You'll get a promotion out of it, I can just about promise you.' Benton bobbed his head and closed the door.

Mike got up and put his hat on. He was moving slowly around the desk when he said, 'It'll be spectacular all right. It may not be spectacular in exactly the way the Commissioner wants, but it'll be spectacular all right. Suppose you drop me off on your way out to Madison's. I'll use my personal car for this job. It's at home.'

'Okay, but first let's risk making Golda wait a few minutes and run past the immigration bureau. I want to know about those fingerprints before I go out to Sherwood Valley with Mallory.'

The immigration people were unruffled and unhurried. A police credential was neither an inspiration or a novelty to them, they were sluggishly efficient, but in due time Paul and Mike were escorted to the cubicle of the head jailer. Behind his fleshy back were twin rows of immaculate white steel cages. The basement atmosphere was cool, but unpleasantly heavy with a scent of disinfectant. The head jailer listened to Paul's explanation of their purpose, got up and told them to wait in his tiny office. Several minutes later he returned with a sallow, dark-eyed man of indeterminate age and unhappy expression. Paul motioned toward the only unoccupied chair in the room and the big jailer leaned in the doorway watching, and saying nothing.

'*Hable Englis?*'

'*Si, Señor;* I went to school here.'

'What is your name?'

'Manuel Torres, *Señor.*'

'Manuel, I'm a police officer. This man here is also a police officer.'

'I understand, yes; there have been other policemen here today, but I swear I have done nothing wrong.'

'No?' said the jailer dryly, 'what do you call illegal entry?'

Torres shrugged, his sharp, tight-skinned face creasing into an apologetic little grin. 'I am expected to do this, *Señores.* I don't do it to hurt anyone, only to get work, to eat and keep my soul alive. It is a natural thing.'

'Torres,' Paul said after studying the

73

pleasant, open—if uneasy—countenance. 'I want to ask you to help the police. Will you do it?'

Torres spread his hands in eloquent agreement. 'But certainly. I have done nothing—I obey the laws—but a man must live, *Señores,* I will—'

'All right; you were fingerprinted this morning weren't you?'

'Yes; the men left only a little while ago.'

Paul jerked his head at Mike, who asked permission to use the telephone on the jailer's desk. When it was granted he called headquarters. Paul continued his interrogation.

'The reason for that was to make sure you are the man who stole a car belonging to a man named Mallory.'

Torres' face twisted into an expression of protest. 'I did not steal the machine. I did only what a man paid me to do. If I had known there would be trouble I would not have gone close to that car. I obey the laws, *Señor,* I am not a criminal.' He waved a hand toward the big jailer. 'Ask him; ask if I have a bad record here. He knows me.'

Paul looked up at the jailer who was grinning crookedly. 'Funny things about these birds,' the jailer said not unkindly. 'They use us as references all the time. He's right; so far as our records show he's never been in any serious trouble—no knife fights, shootings, marijuana. He's just a chronic border-jumper.'

74

'That's fine,' Paul said to Torres. 'Now to get back to that car. Did you take it?'

'Yes, I took it. I was paid to take it. A thousand dollars I was paid. This man said he owned the car.' Torres shrugged. 'I don't ask why a man wants his own car taken away, you can understand that, *Señores.*' Another shrug. 'In this country people do not always make sense to me. If I asked them all why do you do this—or that—would they tell me? I don't think so.'

'So this man paid you a thousand dollars to drive his car away at three in the morning?'

'Yes; he showed me where the car would be—in his driveway with the keys in it. He then gave me one thousand dollars. I would have taken the car for a hundred dollars but he gave me a thousand.'

'Did he say why he wanted you to take the car?'

'No, *Señor.* All he said was for me to drive it up the coast four or five miles beyond the city limits and leave it.'

'I see. Now Manuel, would you know this man again if you saw him?'

'I would know him, yes. *Señor*—I didn't want to break the law. I don't want to lose the thousand dollars either.' Torres hunched up his shoulders and made a wide, disarming smile. 'With this money I can buy a lawyer to get a citizen's papers. I can become an American. But I have been told if I break the

75

law I cannot become a citizen. Do you understand?'

'I understand,' Paul said. 'I don't think you broke a law, Manuel.' He looked up at the jailer again. 'Suppose I have the District Attorney's office put a hold on him for a few days?'

The jailer shrugged. 'Suits me, but you'll have to clear it upstairs. He's scheduled to go back tomorrow. Not that that means a hell of a lot; we fly 'em back one day, the next day they're crawling under the fence again. Still, I know this one; he doesn't get smart or troublesome.'

'Would you go reference for him at a citizenship trial?'

'I guess so. Sure—why not,' the jailer said.

When Mike replaced the telephone Paul asked him what the Lab had said. Mike lit a cigarette. 'They said the prints match perfectly and Torres is our man.'

'All right. Now Manuel, here's what we're going to do. We'll ask that you be detained here until we can get authorisation to have you transferred to the city jail. That's for your own protection. Then we'll want you to positively identify the man who hired you to take that car up the coast and abandon it. Do you understand; can you do that?'

'I can do it. I would know that man's face as sure as I would know yours tomorrow, *Señor*.'

Paul stood up. 'We'll see you again,

Manuel.' He thanked the jailer and led Mike up the stairs to the floor-level offices. 'Call Cap Benton, Mike. Tell him we need Torres. Ask him if he can't get the Commissioner to pull some strings and have him taken to city jail today—right now—we'll take him back with us.'

Mike protested. 'You're going to be late at Madison's.'

it can't be helped. I think this is more important anyway. We need an identification of Mallory, Mike; we need that more than anything which might turn up out at that ruin.'

While Mike was calling in Paul saw the legal head of the immigration bureau, explained why he wanted Torres and was gratified at the co-operation he got, something not always in evidence between Federal and State authorities. Mike no sooner located Paul in the legal department than a call was transferred from the Federal Immigration Bureau's chief to its legal section directing that a prisoner named Manuel Torres be released to the city policemen upon the personal request of the local Commissioner of police.

They returned to headquarters with Torres. Mike stayed with him while he was booked, photographed and assigned to tank-row. Paul left them at the registration desk to seek a picture of Patrick Mallory which he located after considerable effort in an old year-book of the legal profession in the obsolete records section. Torres took a long look at the photograph.

'That's the man,' he said, 'who gave me the thousand dollars and showed me where the machine was.'

Paul returned the year-book and found Mike waiting for him in the corridor. 'Two witnesses,' he said to Mike. 'Levin's and ours. We've got enough to arrest two men, Mike, one for murder, the other for complicity—only the knot around Mallory's not tight enough yet.'

'But I don't mind telling you,' Karger said, 'it's a real relief—the way this worked out.' He glanced at the clock overhead near the bank of elevators. 'Golda's going to be frothing at the mouth—you'd better shove off.'

'Right away. One thing, Mike; before you go out to plant the bug see if something can be done towards getting an audit or an accounting, or something pretty close to the facts about Patrick Mallory's financial situation. Call Sam; if there's an undercover way to do it he'll know.'

Mike blinked. 'I thought he was rich?' he said.

'He may be, but the closer we get to tying him to a murder the more we're going to have to show a motive.'

'Okay,' Mike said, 'see you later.'

The drive to Golda Madison's apartment was through light traffic and a heavy heat haze

78

which was depressing and sticky. When he crossed the patio, skirted the fish-pond and sprang up the little ornamental steps and rapped on the door, he wasn't surprised when Pat Mallory appeared in the opening. He wasn't surprised at Mallory's affability, either.

'Mr. Brewster . . .'

'Good afternoon. Sorry I'm late, but you know how it is . . . Last minute things.'

'Of course. Golda'll be out in a minute. Mix you a drink?' Mallory's normally crisp look was somewhat wilted. His glance was direct and friendly, his tanned face handsome. He was attired in cream coloured slacks and an open-throated sports shirt. 'Found Drexler's killer yet?'

'No drink, thanks.' Paul said moving toward a chair facing away from the windows. 'I'm afraid Drexler's killer isn't going to be so easy to find.'

'No?' Mallory said. 'Well; between us it's no great loss.'

'Possibly not but that's not the point.'

'Of course it isn't, I understand. A man's been killed and a murderer is loose.'

Golda came in looking particularly attractive and cool. He apologised again for being late. She accepted it with a smile and said she hadn't been quite ready either so it really didn't matter, then she looked at Pat Mallory. 'Are we all ready now?' she asked him. 'Shall we go?'

79

Mallory wanted to take his convertible. His reason was that he knew the way. Paul slid in beside Golda and Mallory swung away from the kerb. The ride was pleasant and Mallory kept a running conversation going. Paul watched landmarks and distances, fixing in his mind their route and direction.

An hour later, wind-whipped but at their destination Mallory locked his car at the foot of a brushy slope and jutted his chin towards a faintly discernible footpath winding upwards under the hazy overhang of a land-swell. 'A mile or so of that,' he said to Paul. 'Why don't you leave your tie and coat here? It'll be pretty warm hiking.' Paul did remove his necktie but retained his coat. Mallory started off ahead of Golda and Paul was the last one up the trail. The sun bore down and the still air seemed weighted and a heavy and tangy scent.

After some little distance Mallory showed signs of tiring. He stopped frequently to admire the view and mop his face. Paul was not deceived. When at last they bore around the flank of an especially tall hill Paul saw it standing alone and with an aura of timelessness. The walls were adobe, almost three feet thick which accounted for its durability, and slanted inwards a little as though the forgotten designers had intended to make climbing virtually impossible. The corners were worn smooth and round and where the crooked little path ran out upon the trodden and dusty clearing around the ruin, there arose a sort of battlement which was higher than the rest of the walls, which faced south-west. Conceivably there had been other battlements, but if so, time, winter torrents and centuries of wind had crumpled them. Also, there had once been hovels of some kind beyond the massive walls for stubs of rammed earth jutted here and there among the spiny growth of brush. Mallory stopped in the clearing with sunlight dancing around him and stared long and hard at the ruin. After a time he led them inside and Paul was pleasantly surprised to find how contrastingly cool it was. Cool and dingy.

'The walls are three feet thick even yet,' Mallory said. 'After centuries of weathering. I imagine it was always pretty temperate, too; not too cold in the winter and always this cool in the summer. When I was a boy we used to come out here and dig for buried treasure.' He was smiling at Paul. 'There used to be all sorts of legends about this place. Of course no one actually knows who built it—just Indians and supposedly three or four hundred years ago.' He moved his head in the direction of the lone battlement. 'It is reasonable to assume that they had enemies living along the beaches and were frequently attacked by them. That would account for that battlement or watchtower. Later, Spaniards are said to have buried gold around here. Still later all manner of outlaws frequented the place. Naturally stories sprang up—you know how those legends begin and grow.'

'Is it a popular picnic spot, Mr. Mallory?'

'Well, no, not exactly a popular spot because not many of the late-comers know about it, but it's a secluded and pleasant place and quite often you'll find people up here.'

'Did Drexler know about it?'

Mallory shook his head. 'No; coming up here was my idea. Hugo wasn't interested in things like this—or picnics either, for that matter. I'd told Golda about the ruin. She'd said quite often she'd like to see it.'

'I see. Well, I'd rather stay in here where it's cool, but I'd like to see the spot Drexler fell from.'

Mallory was turning towards some crumbling earthen steps when Golda said, 'I'll wait here.' She smiled apologetically.

Paul followed Mallory up the old steps and thought to himself they were probably a later addition. When he cleared the crumbling roof and emerged into the clear, bright sunlight, heat rolled in and smote him almost physically. Mallory was standing there squinting into the distance. He raised an arm to indicate the lift and fall of land.

'I'd guess that hundreds of years ago the tower offered a fair point of observation. It would have been higher then. I don't imagine the land has altered very much since those days; the people here would be able to see enemies coming long before they got close.' The handsome, tanned face swung towards Paul. 'Wouldn't you rather imagine it to be something like that?'

Paul said he thought it likely, then gazed down from the parapet. The clearing had a certain amount of rubble in it, pieces of shattered adobe, the customary refuse left by treasure hunters and picnickers, but no sharp stones or jagged stumps. 'Is this the spot he fell from?' he asked.

'Over here.' Mallory walked lithely along the wide wall, stopped north-east of the tower and pointed downwards. 'That's where he landed and this is about where he fell from.'

Paul turned and gazed back towards the steps. It would be difficult for a man standing where Drexler had been not to have heard or seen someone approaching him along the parapet. He moved his feet a little, there was no sound of leather upon the abrasive surface, but in spite of that he did not believe Drexler could have been slipped up on, and dismissed the idea that importance should be attached to the fall insofar as subsequent developments were concerned—at least direct developments.

'Seems odd he'd have slipped off a surface as wide as this, doesn't it?' Mallory said.

'It happens like that every day,' Paul replied.

Mallory lit a cigarette, flipped the spent match over the edge and said. 'I can't believe his fall and his death had any connection, Mr. Brewster.' He flagged downwards with the hand holding his cigarette. 'If he'd contemplated suicide he certainly wouldn't try to consumate it here—the fall's not far enough.'

'Why should he contemplate suicide?'

Mallory looked around. 'I have no idea. I simply used it as something to base his fall—or jump—upon. Isn't it obvious to you there could be nothing significant to the fall?'

'No, it's not obvious. I don't believe it had anything to do with his murder, but I'm not closing my mind to some connection either.'

'Did you read last night's papers?'

'About the witness to the Gino Kapelli killing?'

'Yes. Isn't it obvious that Drexler saw that murder and was killed to keep him from identifying the murderer?'

'It would seem that way.'

Mallory turned fully to face Paul. A trace of his characteristic impatience was evident. '*Seem* that way,' he said sharply. 'For two weeks the police have been saying they had a secret witness to Kapelli's murder. Last night, after Drexler was killed, they admitted he was their witness.'

Paul fixed his gaze on a distant pattern of pale green that might have been a mowed hayfield when he replied. 'I'm not on the Kapelli case, Mr. Mallory, I'm on the Drexler murder.'

'You co-ordinate information, don't you?' Mallory was looking at him hard.

'Yes,' Paul said blandly, still gazing off into the distance, 'we co-ordinate it, but Drexler was killed something like thirty hours or so ago—murders take time to clear up.'

Mallory followed Brewster's gaze out over the countryside. The cigarette drooped from his lips and his profile was calm enough except for a shade of impatience. When Paul least expected it he said, 'Look, Brewster—the other day at my place—I caught the unspoken innuendo about the telephone. I can explain that very easily. As an attorney I've had quite a lot of dealings with the police department and I've found that the surest way to get results is to seek them in person.'

'I didn't attach any significance to the telephone,' Paul prevaricated easily. 'People react differently. Anyway, it wouldn't make much difference whether you 'phoned in or called personally.'

'Alibi-wise it would.'

'Yes, alibi-wise it would,' Paul said, 'and I suppose a motive could be attached too, but it'd be a weak one.'

'What motive?' Mallory demanded, swinging to stare at Paul.

'Miss Madison.'

Mallory spat out his cigarette. 'Weak one is right,' he said. 'Golda and I broke up months

85

before she met Drexler. She can tell you that.'

'She already has. She also told me you and Drexler weren't on speaking terms on the way back from here, after he fell off the wall.'

Mallory mopped his forehead and neck with his handkerchief again. 'That is an implication, Brewster. She *thought* we weren't speaking; attached significance to something she imagined. Golda's emotional—I know her much better than you do. She put weight on something she imagined. Haven't you ever driven through a summer afternoon and felt no compulsion to keep a conversation alive?'

'Lots of times,' Paul agreed, and shifted his stance a little. 'I thought it might be partially her imagination.'

Mallory lit another cigarette, frowned at it. 'That's a red herring, there's absolutely nothing to it. What stumps me is this business about Hugo witnessing Kapelli's murder. Granted that he did witness it—which isn't improbable—I can't for the life of me see him voluntarily identifying a murderer for the police department.'

'Why not; it happens every week or so. Kapelli was shot right under his windows. It would have been the most natural thing under the sun for Drexler to look out, see the driver of the murder-car, and call us.'

'No; not Hugo Drexler. If he'd seen something like that he'd be far too wise to say anything about it. It just doesn't fit the kind of a man he was, Brewster. Another thing—why did it take the murderer so long to get around to killing him?'

'The department kept his identity a secret.'

Mallory shook his head. 'I don't buy that,' he said. 'Do you know what I think? I don't think there ever was a witness; I believe the police department engineered the entire thing in order to force someone's hand—make Kapelli's killer come out into the open.'

Paul studied the tanned face a moment. 'You're saying we deliberately let Drexler get killed, Mr. Mallory.'

'I didn't mean *deliberately*. I meant it worked out that way. He wouldn't be the first police witness who was killed you know.'

Paul's gaze was ironic. Mallory was stating a conclusion the department shared, only *they* felt Mallory had engineered it and *he* was saying the department had: *Someone* had set Drexler up to be killed.

'Mr. Mallory—assuming you're right—assuming the department had no actual witness—you know better than to think we'd point Drexler out as the witness.'

'I said I didn't mean you did that deliberately.'

'We didn't do it at all. Why should we; we'd never heard of Hugo Drexler until he was killed. There are two sides to this, Mallory; what we'd like to know is why the underworld thought Drexler was our witness. They'd have to have something pretty positive to kill him. Someone had to pick him out of that entire neighbourhood and finger him to the Kapelli killers.'

Mallory dropped his cigarette, crushed it beneath his shoe and spoke without looking up. 'All right; then it must have been like you said originally—Drexler *must* have been the witness.'

'But you knew him very well and you say it wasn't like the man to be an informer.'

Mallory threw out his hands. 'I give up,' he said. 'Let's go downstairs it's too damned hot up here.'

Paul followed him down the steps and said, 'It'll come out when Kapelli's killer is picked up.'

Mallory said nothing. Golda looked up quickly when they approached and Paul saw how she lingered in her study of Mallory. 'Beautiful view from up there,' he said agreeably. 'Someday I'm going to come up here with my camera.' Golda made no comment but Mallory's next remark showed he had put aside the thoughts he had shared with Paul on the parapet.

'You know, Brewster, what's most remarkable about this ruin is that the Coast Indians were not builders. I don't suppose you knew that, but it's a fact, and that more than anything else is what's stumped archaeologists and naturalists. A building like this is found nowhere else in the State; in fact the only others like it are thousands of miles south-east from here, in some of the early pueblo settlements.'

They passed a pleasantly cool hour in the deep shade of the old ruin's interior then Golda suggested that they had better start back. Mallory led down the trail again and Paul followed Golda. By the time they got to Mallory's car he was damp with perspiration. The drive back to town was exhilarating. A great red sun mantled the hills and a shade of softest pink lay over the land. No one spoke much. At Golda's apartment he thanked them both, declined an invitation to come up, and drove slowly back downtown towards headquarters.

Mike wasn't in the office when he got back. There were no notes or slips indicating telephone calls on his desk so he went back downstairs, ate at the restaurant across from headquarters then drove to his apartment, took a shower and dressed in fresh clothing before returning to his office again.

Sitting by the window thinking back over his conversation with Mallory he tried to satisfy himself whether Mallory was worried or not and came to the reluctant conclusion that he was not. Of course the underworld tip-off about Mallory engineering Drexler's murder for his own ends had not gotten back to those who had been fooled yet, either, and upon that depended much.

The door opened and closed. When no one spoke Paul twisted in his chair. Mike was dabbing at his face with a handkerchief.

'Get it done, Mike?'

'Yup, got it done. No warrant for me on breaking and entering yet, is there?'

Paul turned fully around. 'Are you kidding; you didn't get caught did you?'

Karger crossed the room and threw himself into a chair. He looked uncomfortably hot and dishevelled. 'Didn't get caught,' he said, groping through pockets for a cigarette. 'The earphone's out behind the apartment house in a sort of rose arbour or trellis—or whatever it is. There's a loveseat in there. I hid the bug in some ferns underneath it.' Mike got the cigarette going, blew a gust towards the ceiling. 'If I ever do that in broad daylight again,' he said, 'I hope someone makes me have my head examined.' His eyes dropped. 'What did you turn up?'

'Nothing; had a long conversation with Mallory but Mike, for the life of me I can't figure out whether he's ignorant of what we're up to or just plain cool. I think he's worried about the newspaper stuff about Drexler—but I'm not sure of that, even. He's the slickest one I've ever run across.'

Mike nodded. 'I guess one of us ought to go downstairs and see what Sam's turned up on his financial status, hadn't we?'

'Yes, but let's just talk for a while.'

'Suits me. I feel like I been in a steambath. Man but it's hot out this afternoon.'

There was a lull. The scream of a siren down in the yard broke it. Tyres squealed as a police ambulance hurtled out into the traffic and race southward.

'The next thing we need,' Paul said when the racket had diminished, 'is Drexler's killer.'

'Yeah. If he'd identify Mallory like the wet-back did, we wouldn't have any case—but he won't because he don't know Mallory.'

Paul stood up. 'Be back in a little while,' he said, and left the office. Mike didn't move, his eyes were heavy and half closed.

Downstairs in the accountant's little office Paul drew up a chair. The burly man laid aside his spectacles, rubbed his eyes and let the withered arm lie in his lap. 'You want to know about this Mallory guy Mike called in about, don't you?' he said. Paul nodded. 'Well; here's a simple one. To start with Mallory's not a moneyed man.' Paul drew up a little in his chair. 'He's had money—inherited it I guess—but he's just about shot his wad. His accounts indicate he lives from hand to mouth—in good style but still from hand to mouth.'

'He's got a good legal practice hasn't he?'

Sam made a sour face and shook his head. 'Not so good,' he said. 'He plays around too much, it looks like to me. Sure, he gets a big fee now and then but they're too far between.

This guy lives it up, Paul. Another thing, when he makes investments they usually turn sour. He has no gift along that line. Some of his money I can't trace; apparently he gets it in cash and deposits it the same way. There's nothing illegal here unless you can check out his sources and find them to be so, but it seems odd to me that someone would pay him in cash. Customarily, when big payments are made, people use cheques. Not only for a permanent record, Paul, but also so's they can verify the expenditure when they claim income tax exemption.'

'Unless it's shady.'

The accountant nodded. 'That's probably it. The Lord knows you and I run across enough of that to suspect people of it, anyway.'

Paul got up. 'Is your information sound, Sam?'

'As good as his banker,' Sam said. 'In strictest confidence of course.'

'Sure. This is a surprise,' Paul said. 'I thought he was well padded, Sam.'

'Look,' the accountant said leaning far back in his chair. 'I've been through enough audits exactly like his to make a guess for you. I'll give you odds the Treasury Department is looking into him right now or will be very shortly. He's made some colossal boners in his figures, Paul. The T-men live off guys like this Mallory.'

Paul thanked him and wandered out into

the corridor. He was digesting what he'd learnt as he strolled through the walkway and with finances entering the picture another idea was forming up in his mind.

'Hey, Paul.'

He turned, waited for the hurrying figure to catch up. 'Hello, Bob. What's new?'

'That's what I was going to ask you. Got anything on Mallory yet?'

'A little. A witness that he paid someone to steal his car. How about you—got Clampetti yet?'

Levin swore. 'He's dropped,' he said. 'Just plain dropped. There isn't a feeler who can find him. Know what it looks like to me? Like someone's thinking one jump ahead of you; like they figured Clampetti might do something silly and hid him away but good.'

Paul stared at Levin. 'I hope you're wrong,' he said fervently. 'I hope like all hell you're wrong, Bob.'

'Me too, but how could he fade so good?'

'Skipped the country maybe. Did you get out a poster on him?' Levin nodded. Paul inhaled and exhaled. 'If you're right—if someone killed him—we're in a real spot.'

'You're telling me this? Listen; I've got every cop downtown watching for him. I got stoolies all over. I got copies of his face posted in every squad car—and at the morgue. I can't remember when I wanted a hood so bad.'

'That's something we overlooked,' Paul said

thoughtfully. 'The *killer* might get killed.'

'And where would your case against Mallory be then—the same place ours against Clampetti would be,' Levin said. 'Then what happens? The newspapers find out, the Commissioner finds out . . .'

Paul stopped him with a gesture. 'It hasn't happened yet, Bob. There's still enough to clear us of a persecution or defamation suit.'

'Suit be damned,' Levin said. 'If your Mallory's knocked off our Clampetti, two cases get blown sky-high.'

'*Your* case does,' Paul agreed, 'but not ours. We'd just have another—and better—rap against him, and that would be one time he couldn't have the police force to alibi for him because he'd take care of this one personally—if he did it, which I doubt very much. As he said about Drexler, "he isn't the type" Bob.'

Levin groaned. 'It takes a type to commit murder? You know better, Paul. It takes desperation, fear, hatred, but not a type. Even a coward can be a killer.'

'I won't argue. I know what the extension courses teach, but I also know that there *are* men above murder regardless of the motives inside them. That's not going to help us get Clampetti though, Bob, and right now we want him more than we want Mallory.'

'Another thing I thought about,' Levin said. 'Did you put out the tip about Mallory steering the killer on to Drexler?'

94

'Yes.'

'So—if Mallory hasn't plugged Clampetti what makes you think Clampetti won't kill Mallory?'

'I have no way of knowing he won't,' Paul answered, 'but I also spread the rumour that Clampetti's after Mallory, in such a way Mallory'll hear it with only half an effort.'

'And?'

'I think Mallory's going to come screaming to us for protection. I already explained that to you.'

'Yeah, but has he come yet?'

'He hasn't had time. Look; you and Herb just dig up Anthony Clampetti, get him locked up and I'll sweat Mallory out.'

He left Levin standing in the hallway, went back to the office and Mike greeted him with a yellow call-slip. 'Golda,' he said.

Paul dropped down at his desk, put a hand on the telephone, but made no effort to raise it. 'Mallory's broke, Mike. All that big front is phoney. He gets sizeable amounts of money from some unknown source in cash every once in a while, and Sam intimated he's juggling his income tax records.'

'Broke?' Mike said incredulously. 'Living like he does, driving new cars, dressing fit to kill—how could he be broke?'

'How he got that way doesn't interest me,' Paul replied. 'It's enlightening to know there might be another angle to this.'

'You better button up the ones you got already before developing any new ones,' Mike said.

Paul acted as though he hadn't heard. 'I want you to go downstairs and see what you can dig up on Mallory's clients. He's bound to have a few hoodlums retaining him from time to time. And listen—do this without Rasch or Levin knowing you're doing it—file-search for friends, relatives, acquaintances of Anthony Clampetti.'

'That's their job,' Mike said, but he got up and lumbered towards the door. Before passing from sight he said, 'Don't forget to call Golda.' Then he slammed the door.

But Paul called Corte at the District Attorney's office first and Golda second. Corte was interested in what progress had been made in the case. He offered the sound suggestion that before Paul moved to arrest Mallory he double-checked with the legal office to be sure of his grounds. This Paul agreed to and hung up.

Golda sounded languid over the telephone. 'I wish you'd come up for a moment after we got back to my place,' she said. 'I wanted to hear what you'd deduced from the ruin.'

'It wouldn't have taken long to tell you that,' he said. 'Nothing. I don't believe Drexler's fall had anything to do with his murder.'

'I'm relieved,' she said.

'Why?'

96

'Well; I was there when he fell, you know.'

'I never implied you were under suspicion; for that matter I never implied Mallory was either.'

'Don't you have a suspect then?'

'Yes, we have a suspect,' he said, and volunteered nothing more. Mike Karger entered the office, hesitated when he saw Paul at the telephone, then closed the door very softly.

'. . . Talked it over after we got back. Pat doesn't think the police are going about it right. He seems to believe Hugo's murderer had a robbery motive or something like that. Isn't it possible he's right?'

'Very possible,' Paul said, and winked aside at Mike. 'Time will tell. Was there anything in particular you wanted me for?' She said no and he hung up, tilted back in his chair and swivelled around. 'You couldn't look so happy and not have something good,' he said to Mike. 'What is it?'

'Herb Rasch just called Levin from uptown. He's got a hot tip about Clampetti.'

Relief flooded Paul and he relaxed in the chair. 'Is Bob going out?'

'Yes; he asked me to find out if you want to go along.'

'Like Eisenhower to Gettysburg,' Paul said arising.

'Let's go.'

They caught Levin just as he was leaving his

office. The crinkly-haired detective looked
breathless without being that way. He jerked
his hand at them and hurried down the
corridor towards the vestibule. Beyond was
night, something Paul wasn't aware of, and a
rash of blue-white stars pimpled the sky's
underbelly. He glanced hastily at his watch
then hurried after Bob Levin. Mike, trailing
after, said something unpleasant but no one
heeded him. Just before they piled into Levin's
car Mike shoved a paper into Paul's hand.

'The dope you wanted on Mallory,' he said,
jack-knifed into the rear seat and bumped his
head, swore, re-creased his hat and went on,
'Sam had the report on his finances finished so
I picked that up too. It's there with the others.'

Paul glanced briefly at the papers then over
at Bob Levin. 'Where is he?' he asked.

'Herb's down there watching the place. It's
bona fide too; he saw him himself.' Levin
burnt rubber leaving the kerb and Paul made
no further attempt to pump him, but began
reading the report on Mallory. When he got to
the financial report for the previous year he
puckered up his mouth in a silent whistle.

'Something's beginning to make sense,
Mike,' he said.

'You mean the eighty-eight thousand
Mallory dropped on the stock market? I read
that, too.'

'It doesn't figure. Did you look at the
income bracket; he doesn't have that kind of

98

money to lose.'

'I know. Look at the bank balances at the bottom of the page. From a quarter of a million down to forty-four thousand.'

Paul shuffled the pages so that the income sheet was arranged beside the expenditure columns. Mallory had made only a little over thirty thousand at his law practice. He folded the pages and placed them into an inside pocket, was staring past the windscreen at the lighted city when Bob Levin looked around, saw that he was unoccupied, and spoke.

'Herb's pet stoolie 'phoned him at home where Clampetti was. A joint called the "Aloha" down on the Miracle Mile. Herb went down, made a stake-out and sure enough, he saw our boy.'

'The Miracle Mile?' Mike said. 'That's pretty high-class for a character like Clampetti, Bob.'

'What else? Look; we been dragging the tenderloin, his natural habitat, and where's he turn up? That was pretty smart. You'll never convince me Clampetti had the brains to figure that one out. I'll never believe he had the contacts to get a hide-out there either.' Levin grew silent as he swung south into the blaze of multi-coloured neon signs that washed the pavement with their brilliance, sat hunched over the wheel peering for one that said Aloha.

'You got the number?'

'No, but I know where it is. Down there at the bottom of the hill somewhere; lots of ritzy nightclubs down there.'

'You ever met this Clampetti before, Bob?'

'No, but I've been sleeping with his image in my mind long enough now to know him on sight. He's a torpedo, too—don't get careless.'

A black and white patrol car whizzed past them with its flasher light sending out jolts of dazzling red light. Mike looked up in surprise, watched it weave in and out of the traffic and swore. 'Why doesn't he hit the siren,' he said. Paul and Bob watched the squad car without commenting. When it dipped from sight Paul began reading neon signs again.

'We're going to run out of area pretty quick,' he said to Bob Levin.

A long way off the wail of a siren rose to a crescendo, quivered there then dropped away to begin its climb again. Levin slowed and craned his neck to see behind them. Traffic was veering away from the road's centre as the siren came closer. 'Travelling fast,' he said to no one in particular and decelerated, easing out of the main traffic lane. 'Fine night for trouble, it looks like.'

They let the ambulance hurtle past then Levin flicked on their red flasher light and worked his way down towards the base of the hill. Traffic was heavy; they were in a part of town where people ate out on Thursday nights. Paul lit a cigarette, inhaled deeply and the red glow made his eyes glisten redly inside the car. 'See it yet, Mike.'

'No.'

Quite suddenly Bob Levin stiffened in his seat and threw out his arm. 'There it is.' Paul and Mike sought the sign, found it and were opening doors to alight almost before Levin had the car stopped.

'And there's something else, too,' Mike said. 'That squad car that went past us back up the hill.'

He was only partly correct, for when they started to cross through the traffic they could see two black and white departmental machines. One was slanted towards the kerbing as though its occupants had left it hastily. It's flasher light was blinking on and off. The car was partially obstructing traffic.

'Something's going on,' Paul said, uneasiness mounting in him.

A grey-dark and shapeless mob of people were standing motionless beneath the inappropriately gay neon sign announcing the Aloha nightclub, and from beyond a palomino door farther up the street came strains of music. A policeman was using his arms to compel the onlookers to get back from the edge of the street. Mike touched Paul's arm, nodded towards something dark in the road near where the grey ambulance was edging through a skein of cars. 'Accident,' he said.

A large policeman in a freshly pressed

uniform watched them cut diagonally across the street, his brows settled low and he called to them. Paul was first to reach his side.

'What's the matter you guys—want to get killed? There's laws against jay-walking like that.'

Paul flicked his I.D. folder then pocketed it. 'What happened?' he asked mildly.

'Dead guy—there. That's all I know—just got here. There's a headquarters detective some place around—I saw him just a few minutes ago.'

Paul turned to walk toward the little group of uniformed policemen talking and taking notes by the headlights of one of the squad cars when he noticed Bob Levin walking rapidly towards the ambulance attendants in white coats and trousers. Mike was with him. Shadows blurred as a man detached himself from the group of uniformed men and hastened toward Levin. Paul was moving forward when he saw Levin drop to one knee beside the blanket-covered corpse, lift a corner and let it drop. He did not get back to his feet. From that distance Paul thought he looked like a man upon whose shoulders someone had just dropped a tremendous weight.

He stopped beside Mike, who was standing in an unnaturally erect fashion watching Levin. Someone brushed past him, it was the attendants with a rubberised stretcher which they put down next to the body. One of them

102

lifted the old blanket and put a dark rubber sheet in its place. During the interim Paul had seen and recognised the dead man. The shock numbed him.

Mike said, 'He got him. He shot Herb.'

Paul moved closer, bent for a closer look and one of the attendants shot him a dark glare. He let the sheet fall back and turned away. There was no doubt, it was Herb Rasch all right.

The uniformed men were moving among the spectators. Paul could see them shake their heads in dogged silence. It angered him. 'Someone saw it!' he said harshly, and checked himself. Seeking witnesses was a waste of time; it didn't matter which side of town they came from, no one ever saw a killing. Mike moved towards the uniformed men. He spoke softly as he swung past Paul.

'His gun's in its holster. He never touched it. Right over the heart, Paul.'

He turned to look back where Levin was. Rasch's partner was leaning against the side of the ambulance. An attendant was talking earnestly to him. Levin appeared not to be listening, his face was averted.

Why, Paul asked himself. They'd actually had nothing but suspicion; the killer must have known that, so why—this? There was nothing in Clampetti's rap-sheet to indicate he was an addict—then why had he killed Rasch? It didn't make sense. For one thing Herb Rasch was a seasoned detective; he wouldn't make his stake-out so obvious Clampetti would see him. How had it happened? He watched the uniformed men trying to get information from the onlookers, watched Mike filtering among the crowd asking questions, getting shrugs and negative headshakes. It didn't matter. Ten witnesses wouldn't confirm what he knew; Herb Rasch was dead, shot through the heart by Anthony Clampetti wanted for questioning in connection with two murders. It didn't matter *how* Clampetti had known Rasch was a detective so much as it mattered that Rasch was dead.

The crowd was thinning out. He saw Mike returning towards him from the crowd. The way Mike was walking told the story of his failure to locate a witness. Paul lit a cigarette and waited, heard the dismal grind of the ambulance's siren as the machine moved out into the swirl of traffic.

'No one saw it,' Mike said. 'The harness cops put a dragnet around the block. I called for Cap Benton to get an A.P.B. out on Clampetti as a cop-killer. A couple of the squad men questioned the bartender at the Aloha, the waitresses and the manager.' Mike lifted a hand and let it fall. 'Nothing. No one remembers Herb—no one saw anything suspicious—and if I had a picture of Clampetti twenty feet square no one would remember ever having seen him.'

Paul looked a little past Mike's shoulder as he listened. Clampetti would go into hiding now like he'd never done before. It was the department's boast that no one had ever shot a cop and gotten away with it. The underworld would shun the cop-killer like he was a leper. His shoulders sagged.

CHAPTER FOUR

'Did you get the Aloha's owner's name?'

'Sabellis,' Mike said. 'They've already talked to him, he said he was inside and didn't hear anything.'

'Who discovered Herb?'

'A couple of kids passing in a sports car.' Mike motioned towards a squad car. 'They're going to go downtown and make a statement.'

'Let's go inside.'

The mob was idling away. There was some talk, not much, as they shouldered past and into the nightclub. A heavy aroma of liquor, perfume, and tobacco smoke met them. Paul caught a frozen-faced busboy.

'Where's Mr. Sabellis's office?'

'Through there, sir. Beyond the dining-room; the door on the far side with the gold star in the middle of it.'

The Aloha had a few desultory diners but most of the tables showed evidence of hasty

105

departures. The bar-room was totally empty. A waitress looked up quickly then averted her face, became busy over an empty tray.

Paul jolted the door with a fisted set of knuckles and gazed dispassionately at the golden star. A man swung the door inward almost at once.

'Is your name Sabellis?'

'It is. Come in.' Sabellis closed the door and stood with his back to it.

'We're police officers.'

'I thought as much,' Sabellis said. He was short, massive, clean shaven and dark eyed. 'It's about that killing isn't it?' He motioned toward chairs. 'I've already been asked what I knew. The answer is—nothing. I was here, in my office. Until I heard the commotion of people leaving in a hurry—chairs pushed back, loud talking—I had no idea anything had happened. A waitress came to the door and told me . . .'

'How long has Anthony Clampetti been hiding out here, Sabellis?' Paul shot at him.

'Mr. Detective—I swear—I did not know either of those men. Which one was Clampetti?'

'The killer. The dead man was a city detective. Sabellis—level with us. You're not going to walk out of this, but the truth might help.'

Sabellis' liquid dark eyes widened. 'I'm telling you the exact truth,' he said. 'I didn't

106

know either of those men—didn't even know what had happened until sometime afterwards. I have never known anyone named Clampetti and no one's been hiding at the Aloha.' He gestured towards the expensive furnishings of the office. 'This isn't a dive, officer. Listen to me—I'm absolutely respectable. I ask you to investigate me—my family, my friends, my business associates.'

Paul removed Clampetti's rap-sheet from his pocket, held it out. 'We'll investigate you all right. Here; did you ever see that man before, any time, anywhere?'

Sabellis' moved closer, squinted at the tiny picture and straightened up, took a long cigar from an inside pocket and held it unlighted in one hand. 'He's an absolute stranger to me,' he said, and when Paul's gaze didn't waver Sabellis gestured with the unlighted cigar. 'I'd tell you, believe me I would. What has this man done to me tonight? Ruined my business—perhaps not only for tonight. These people—they aren't going to forget a detective was killed outside my door.' The gesturing cigar-hand became more agitated. 'This could close me up, gentlemen.' He stabbed at the photo with his cigar. There was something quick and hating in the movement. 'If I knew this man wouldn't I tell you? I'd be *glad* to if I *ever* see him I'll tell you.'

Paul put the rap-sheet back in his pocket and looked over at Mike. Karger's expression was coldly appraising. He was studying Sabellis like a hawk. Finally he cleared his throat.

'What about your employees? How about bartenders, waitresses, busboys, cooks—do you know if any of them have police records?'

'To my knowledge, no. I would not knowingly hire such a person. My trade is better class. I couldn't risk it.' He squared around to look at Mike. 'You can check them; it's not impossible someone has lied to me. Here,' Sabellis moved around his immense, glass-topped desk. 'Let me show you my employment forms. There, look right there—if they write in that blank space that they have a police record I don't hire them.'

Mike looked at the form and passed it along to Paul. 'How about the completed forms; give me a list of your employees.'

Sabellis laid aside the unlighted cigar and frowningly sifted through a card index. 'Copy them from this officer. The cards with black tabs are the night shift, the others are all day help. Here, sit at my desk.'

While Mike went to work copying the names and information Sabellis re-crossed the room where Paul stood, spread his hands palms up and raised his eyebrows. His face glistened under the pale, indirect lighting. 'I'll help any way that I can. Any way at all. All I want is for you to acknowledge that the Aloha had no connection whatsoever with this affair—after you've completed your investigation. You understand . . .'

'Have you ever been in trouble, Mr. Sabellis? Any police record?'

'Absolutely not—never.'

Sabellis continued speaking, Paul listened without paying very close attention, he felt tired and worn out. When Mike finished the list they both left.

Outside the night was dark, the squad cars were gone and the normal trickle of pedestrian traffic resumed. Mike ambled to a news-stand and bought an evening paper. For a moment he and the proprietor talked then Mike returned.

'He see anything?' Paul asked.

'Thought it was a firecracker. I guess from that there was just one shot.' Mike shook out the paper, glanced at it briefly, folded it and tucked it in a coat pocket. 'What's this going to do to us, Paul,' he said. 'Clampetti'll be as hard to locate as a ghost. The Commissioner and the papers'll be burning the wires for action.'

'I know; I wish I knew.' He glanced unconsciously at the spot where Herb Rasch had been. There was nothing there; cars were driving over it. A man's life had been snuffed out—traffic continued, nothing changed outwardly, the city went on throbbing and writhing. 'Let's find Bob and head back.'

'He must've gone back in the ambulance. Not around.'

They drove back in silence, left Levin's

machine at the kerb and hiked glumly up three flights of stairs. Voices sounded from beyond their door. Paul twisted the knob and pushed. Captain Benton and Corte, the man from the D.A's office, looked up and fell silent. Benton's face was a mask of icy fury.

'Anything?' He shot at them. Paul shook his head and dropped his hat on the desk. Benton's words were like bullets. 'I don't want any sleep around here until he's taken—I don't care *how*—but taken!'

'Have you seen Levin?' Paul asked quietly.

'Yes; he's out with the dragnet. The city's sealed off. I put the reserves in and cancelled vacations. That guy's going to sweat like he never sweated before. He'll never leave this town alive.'

'He won't leave the city anyway,' Paul said wearily, dropping down on a chair. Benton blinked belligerently at him.

'Why won't he? He's a cop-killer isn't he?'

'You can't execute a man but once,' Paul said, returning Benton's stare. 'He's been wanted for questioning in connection with two murders for several days. Do you think another killing's going to make any difference?'

'A cop killing—'

'Cop killing or any other kind,' Paul interrupted shortly with an edge in his voice, 'he didn't run before and he won't now. He's got a good hideout somewhere—somewhere

where the cops won't look. He killed Rasch on the Miracle Mile, an area where hoods are as scarce as lice.'

There was spite more than anger in Benton's reply. 'All right; you've master-minded things so far—this is your case until it's solved. If it takes for ever it's your headache, but it better not take that long. In fact it better not take more'n a week—remember what those primaries can do to the Commissioner.'

When Benton ceased speaking a great hollow silence filled the office. Paul was looking straight into Benton's face and his expression was like granite.

'I don't suppose Herb's family'll care much how those primaries turn out,' he said, and felt around for a cigarette. Mike offered his own package; Mike's blunt, square face was dark with anger, but his mouth was tightly closed. Seeing the antagonism Corte spoke to alleviate it.

'What is your opinion, Mr. Brewster? I mean—you've been watching this thing . . .'

Paul blew smoke out and replied without looking at Corte. 'My opinion is that we've got to nail Mallory first.'

'Mallory!' Benton spat. 'What's—?'

'Yes, Mallory. We're not going to locate Clampetti's hideout. I'll give you any kind of odds on that. Whoever's doing his thinking for him has perfected the hideout technique so

111

well it'd take a city-wide shake-down, house by house, to turn him up. We don't have that much time so we've got to locate him through someone who *knows* where he's hiding. I believe Mallory does; I believe that because after we spread the rumour that Mallory double-crossed Drexler's killer, and Mallory knows he might come after him with a gun; he'll make it a point to know where Clampetti is every minute of the day and night. He can't afford not to know. By now Clampetti's got the word he was used by Mallory; he'll be out to kill his fourth man.' He looked across the room at Corte before resuming. 'Like I said; we can't execute him but once whether he kills one man or four.' Paul got up heavily and moved to his desk aimlessly, looked at the contents of his mail baskets without concentrating on them, sat on the edge of the desk and looked through Captain Benton.

'If we knew how Clampetti knew Rasch was staking him out we'd know enough to pick somebody up.'

Mike said, 'It was a perfect set-up, too. Herb was shot right up close—in the heart. He never saw it coming until it was there—practically in his face. Someone had to have been watching him; someone who knew Rasch on sight but who Rasch didn't know. If it was Clampetti then—'

'It was dark, Mike,' Paul said. 'Maybe Clampetti had a confederate and maybe he recognised Herb, stalked him, and when he saw his shot he took it.' Paul shook his head. 'But why? Clampetti knew he was wanted, sure, but why did he kill a cop when all he had to do was walk away? If he'd spotted Herb then he surely could have gotten away. Why did he kill him?'

Captain Benton ran a thick, hairy hand around inside his shirt collar. 'I don't know why,' he said, 'and I don't care why. I just want this guy dead or alive and preferably dead.'

'Okay,' Paul said flatly. 'Okay. Who is the best stoolie you've got in the underworld, Captain?'

Without hesitating Benton said, 'Sunny Lee.'

'The little pickpocket and numbers mug?'

'The same. What about him?'

'Tell him you've got it straight Clampetti's out to kill Mallory no later than tomorrow night.'

Benton inclined his head. 'All right; but I think you've got enough to drag Mallory in right now, haven't you?'

'Sure, on small counts—and he's an attorney.' Paul glanced at Corte. 'How long would we be able to hold him on misdemeanours?'

'An hour maybe, but didn't you tell me you wanted him on suspicion of murder or being an accessory to murder?'

'Yes; that's what I *want* him for, but there's

113

just not enough evidence to book him like that yet.' He faced Benton again. 'When can you contact your stoolie?'

'Now; any time.'

'The sooner the better; if he got the word around tonight it might do the trick. You can use this phone.'

Benton demurred. 'No, I'd rather make the call from my own place.' He started for the door. 'What're you going to do?'

'Mike's going to check out the employees of a man named Sabellis who owns the night-spot where Rasch was killed. I'm going to look over some reports I haven't had time to go over yet—stuff on Mallory, his clients, finances . . .' He walked around his desk and sat in the chair. 'I also want to get some legal info from Mr. Corte.'

Benton left. Mike Karger looked uncertainly at Paul and fingered the employee list from the Aloha. 'Sabellis too?' he asked. Paul nodded and Mike left the office.

Corte drew his chair closer to the desk and looked up inquiringly. 'What about the legalities?' he asked.

'Look; I know this is illegal as hell, Corte, but nevertheless I've got a bug on Mallory's girl friend's telephone. Now the question is— of course I know evidence gained that way is inadmissible—but what I want to know is whether, in the event Mallory, or his attorney if he has to hire one, finds out about the bug, whether they could ask for a dismissal on charges of police info being obtained illegally.'

'They could,' Corte said instantly, 'and they would. The D.A's pretty much against bugging telephones, Brewster. He might object to filing in a case where it's generally known a bug was used. When we go to court we want a conviction; it doesn't look good for a D.A. to lose cases or get involved in cases where the evidence was gotten illegally.' Corte spread his hands. 'The way to use the bug is by getting evidence you can use to secure better evidence. In other words, let's assume Mallory lets something slip over the phone—you take it from there; use the information to pick him up on a connected charge without ever making reference to your source—follow me?'

'I'm ahead of you. That's what I told Mike we'd use the bug for.' Mike stood up. 'That's all I wanted to know; Mallory's sharp, I don't want to muff this.'

Corte arose. 'No,' he said cryptically, 'after listening to Captain Benton this evening I can understand that. Anything else?'

'Not right now. Thanks; I'll keep you posted. In fact I'll want lots of legal help before this is over with, Mallory's going to be no pushover.'

'You're certain in your own mind he's your man?'

'As sure as I'm standing here.'

'Good,' Corte said with a smile. 'Call me

115

any time. Good night.'

Paul was turning down the corridor when Benton emerged from his own office farther up and called out to him. 'I got it done. The word'll spread like wild-fire; Mallory'll know it by morning at the latest—if he's got an inside tap.'

'Good,' Paul said, and went to the stair-well, down it to Records and Files, found Mike working with a dead cigarette in his lips and his coat off.

'Anything?'

Mike removed the cigarette, threw it down and shook his head. 'That guy was levelling with us. I hate to let him off the hook, but none of them so far have records.'

'I thought he was telling the truth, Mike. Well, I'm for home and some sleep. See you tomorrow morning early.'

'Yeah, early.'

In his apartment Paul threw his coat and tie upon a couch, flung himself into a chair after turning on the electric coffee pot, and lit a cigarette. The sounds of the city came mutedly through the walls. The night was still young but an edge of quiet was discernible too; honest people slept. He made a humourless smile. Golda and Mallory were probably sleeping too; not such honest people, and Anthony Clampetti—no—he wouldn't be sleeping. A man with too-wide-apart eyes, a low, thick forehead, wet marbles for eyes and a

116

cop-murder in his memory—he wouldn't be sleeping. Neither would the hundreds of men seeking him. The Lord help Anthony Clampetti if he poked his nose out tonight.

The coffee spread its delicious aroma through the apartment. He got up, poured a cup and returned to the chair, drank it and promptly fell asleep. The telephone roused him at seven-thirty the following morning. He lifted the telephone and his eyelids at the same time. He felt stiff, cramped, and his mouth tasted like the inside of a bait bucket.

'Brewster here.'

'This is Mike. You over-sleep?'

'I guess so. Anything new yet?'

'No, but Benton's here and the place is humming. The dragnet turned up nothing—as usual. You on your way down?'

'Right away, Mike.'

He hung up, got up, stretched and headed for the shower. Fresh and redressed he drank two quick cups of coffee and left the apartment. A newsy at the corner across from headquarters nailed him with a black headline. 'Paper, mister?' He bought it, cross the street and winced at the bold legend: DETECTIVE MURDERED BY HOODLUM! There was a portrait of Herb Rasch half-size on the front page but details were skimpy. An editorial column stung him with crisp, harsh words. He folded the paper and entered the vestibule, crossed to the stairway and started up.

Captain Benton was just entering the office when Paul swung into the corridor. He looked up and waited, holding the door open.

'Anything turn up yet?'

Benton shook his head without replying and slammed the door behind them. Mike was talking over the telephone. He hung up and nodded. 'Seen the papers, Paul?'

'Yeah.' Paul faced Benton. 'Where's Levin?'

'Out with the squads.'

'All night?'

'Yes, all night,' Benton snapped. 'Now look; we're going to break this today.'

Paul felt resentful and sat down at his desk. 'We've got to have something besides determination to do it with,' he said.

Benton glared. 'We got it.' He waved some crumpled papers. 'Lists of this Clampetti guy's friends. Mike; you take one squad and Paul, you'll take another—you'll both pick them up for questioning as fast as you locate them.'

'Put someone else on that,' Paul said coolly, 'I've got a job for Mike. Another thing, this talk about Clampetti dead or alive: Dead, the department'll be revenged for Rasch, but alive we'll have the answers to three murders. Which way will look the best to the Commissioner?'

Benton's glowering gaze hung on Paul's face. He let the hand holding aloft the list of names drop to his side, but he was silent for a long time. The answer was obvious anyway.

'All right,' he finally said, somewhat subdued in tone, 'alive then.'

'You'd better pass the word,' Paul said. 'I imagine by now every guy working the streets is itching to exercise a trigger finger.'

With much of his fire gone Captain Benton said, 'What about a tail on Mallory?'

Paul shook his head. 'We've got something better than that, but it'd help if you'd check with your stoolies and make sure they spread the word about Clampetti being after Mallory.'

'Can't do that in here,' Benton said moving toward the door. He glanced at the papers in his hand. 'Okay; I'll send someone else after these birds.'

When he was gone Paul turned toward Mike. 'One of us has got to man the bug today, Mike; that's why I wanted to get Benton out of here. Is it safe in daylight?'

'I think so. It's in a sort of secluded corner of the garden. I think a guy could sit still in there and unless someone walked right up, they wouldn't see him. Want me to take it?'

'Yeah; if you don't pick up anything worthwhile and call in, I'll come out after sundown and relieve you. Better pick up some candy bars, it's liable to be a long wait.'

After Mike left Paul went downstairs to the little cubicle of the accountant. 'Sam; I didn't have time to read that report. I thought maybe you could fill me in. I'd understand it better, too, coming from you.'

119

'Sure, sit down.' The accountant removed his glasses, laid them atop some papers and gazed at Paul. 'Were you there when Rasch got it?'

'No; a few minutes afterwards. That's part of this same case, Sam.'

The accountant's eyebrows climbed. 'You mean this Drexler-Mallory business?'

'Yes. Tell me in capsule form what's good and what's bad about those two birds, will you?'

'Sure. Like I told you this Drexler was an operator. I'm sure he's got safety-deposit boxes around somewhere—maybe not in his right name, but I'll bet he's got some. Drexler's been mixed up with the police somewhere, I'll bet on that, he's one of those guys who skimmed awfully close to the edge in his dealings. Not exactly crooked, but shady. How shady only a complete audit would show . . .'

The voice droned on, Paul heard but deep in his mind an idea had stirred, grown, absorbed his deductive processes. Drexler—stock manipulator—Mallory—-eight thousand lost in the market—Golda Madison's financial adviser; large cash deposits to Mallory's account from time to time—Good God!

'I think I've got it, Sam,' he said in the midst of the accountant's detailed explanation of figures and percentages. Sam stopped in mid-sentence and looked at him hard.

'I think I've got the connection, Sam.'

120

'What connection?'

'The one between *why* a man was murdered and *how* he was murdered.'

'I don't get it.'

'A crime's composed of two parts, Sam, the act and the intent. Without the intent a killing can be an accident, but with intent it becomes a murder. In other words, a crime is commission and intent—or the *act* and the *motive*. Until this minute I could not figure out what the motive was—now I think I know.' He got up and smiled. 'See you later, Sam.'

He cut swiftly across the outer lobby, through the doors and around to the Dispatcher's office, got a car and wheeled out into the traffic. Morning sunlight was cutting like a torch, through the city's murk. The drive to Normandie was completed with almost unconscious effort and Golda Madison was at home. She greeted him gravely and closed the door behind him.

'I was shocked about that killing last night,' she said. 'Did you know Detective Rasch?'

'Yes, I knew him.'

'Why was he killed? Who did it?'

'We're only guessing,' he said. 'It's a little early to say, but this much I do know; no one has ever gotten away after killing a city policeman yet. Neither will this man.'

'It was a terrible thing,' she murmured just as a very pretty girl in a plain black dress entered the room, shot Paul a startled glance

121

and while evidently on the verge of saying something, remained silent.

'Breakfast, Betty?'

'Yes'm,' the girl said.

'Thank you I'll be right in.' Golda looked up at Paul. 'Couldn't you join me?'

He acted on the spur of the moment. 'Why don't you join me? There's a place down on the boulevard that serves the best waffles in the city.' At her hesitant expression he arose saying, 'I'd consider it a real favour if you would.' She searched his face a moment before accepting, and after she'd left the room he turned and looked down across the city beyond a tall window. A half-formed notion was firming up in his mind. The approach to it had been lame, but he was committed. When she came back in street clothes she smiled at him.

'I've never gone to breakfast with a policeman before, Mr. Brewster.'

'Nor I with so lovely a woman,' he said gallantly holding the door for her, closing it gently after she passed through and following down across the patio and out to the police sedan. She hesitated there. He opened the door with a quirked-up little grin.

'Maybe the neighbours'll think I'm taking you in.'

She got in and smiled self-consciously but did not speak. They drove south to the first arterial boulevard and went west to a small, immaculate café, had a leisurely breakfast and when the tab came Paul searched his pockets, found himself short and looked genuinely embarrassed when Golda Madison had to write the cheque which he took to the cashier, but folded into the palm of his hand while paying with a bill of his own. He pocketed the cheque, returned to the table, apologised for being out of funds and took her back to the car. She was in a laughing frame of mind when he held open her apartment door for her. He killed an hour in small talk then left, drove a short distance off, parked the car, rummaged through the papers in his pockets for the financial statement on Hugo Drexler, lit a cigarette and studied it for twenty minutes before resuming his way uptown.

Drexler had netted upwards towards a quarter of a million dollars on the stock market over the past two years. The previous year alone his net had been in excess of one hundred thousand dollars. What particularly interested Paul was a withdrawal of sixty thousand dollars from his personal bank account, and another one for twenty-eight thousand dollars, or a total of eighty-eight thousand, withdrawn within the same week. Eighty-eight was the amount Patrick Mallory had lost on the market.

Paul read the expense sheet carefully. The accountant had listed with meticulous thoroughness every expense, even groceries and nightclub costs; nowhere was there any indication of what had become of the eighty-eight thousand dollars.

He parked outside the Southwest Banking and Trust Company, entered and was eventually ushered into the manager's office.

'You have the account here of a Miss Golda Madison,' he said, with her cheque in his hand with the institution's name across the top of it. 'Could I see it unofficially or shall I call the District Attorney's office for a court order, and wait?'

The manager drummed soundlessly on the arm of his chair for a moment, then heaved up out of it. 'I suppose the wait would result in the same thing, wouldn't it. Excuse me a moment.'

Paul lit a cigarette and looked beyond the glassed partition. The bank was crowded. A steady hum of voices and machines rose towards the fluted ceiling. The manager returned with a thick folder and an extra swatch of loose papers. He put them down carefully, ran his finger down a column of figures and said, 'This is the current account, Mr. Brewster. That's her bank balance—a comfortable one.'

'This is the one I'm looking for—here—deposits.' He ran his finger down it and stopped where a deposit of twenty-eight thousand dollars had been made in cash. He compared the date with the Drexler ledger sheet and felt his heart slugging while he did so. The dates were identical. He leaned back in the chair and made a less intense search for a matching withdrawal, and found it dated several weeks prior to the deposit. He got up and extended his hand.

'I'm very much obliged,' he said. 'I appreciate it if you wouldn't mention that a detective was examining these records to Miss Madison.'

The manager looked rueful. 'Not much chance of that,' he said, pumping Paul's hand. 'Say; wasn't that a terrible thing that happened out on the Miracle Mile last night?'

'We think it was,' Paul agreed, and left.

He sat in the car making notations for a moment, then he spread Patrick Mallory's report from the police accountant on one knee and studied it with a vertical crease between the eyes. If his guess was correct there would be a sixty thousand cash deposit to match Golda's twenty-eight thousand dollar deposit. There was.

He drove to a pay-station and called the accountant. 'Sam; I've got to have the name of Patrick Mallory's bank—do you have it?'

'Sure; it should be in the report.'

'It isn't.'

'Okay; just a second.' The line hummed; beyond Paul's kiosk people streamed both ways. 'Here: Security First National, head office on Spring Street.'

'Thanks.' He drove leisurely through the

125

heart of the city, parked and sought an old acquaintance in the Trust Department; a telephone call later he had Mallory's account before him. It tallied with the accountant's figures to the last cent. He left the bank, ate a thoughtful lunch and headed southwest back to headquarters. The accountant didn't look surprised when he entered his office.

'You find something good?' he asked as Paul sat down.

'What I was hoping for. Drexler was Golda Madison's fiance but her ex-boy friend was her financial adviser.'

'That's an odd arrangement,' the accountant said. 'Looks like she didn't have much faith in Drexler's judgment—but from what I know I'd say she was wrong. Was Mallory the boy friend?'

'Yes. Now let's suppose Drexler—whom I know was a vindictive and very clever manipulator—wanted to destroy Golda's faith in Mallory. He could do it because he was much smarter than Mallory. How would he do it?'

'That's not tough; he'd clean him in the market.'

'And I'll bet that's exactly what he did, Sam. Not only cleaned him but got Mallory to invest some of Golda's money in some stock he recommended, so she lost also. That eighty-eight thousand, for instance, tallies out in both their bank accounts. But—and here's the

126

catcher—Drexler made it good. He paid them both back in cash.'

'Oh. That's where the money went. That had me stumped but good.' Sam scratched his head. 'Why? Why—after he'd worked it to humble Mallory—would he make it good? I mean, that's just showing himself up. So Mallory threatened to pin his ears back—if he gave in like a coward it'd make him look pretty poor in the Madison woman's eyes, wouldn't it?'

'Yes, and she told me he might have been a physical coward. That's what was in her mind, Sam, sure as shooting. She was thinking of how Drexler had backed-water for Mallory.' Paul frowned. 'If the money was repaid, would Mallory still consider it sufficient cause to kill Drexler, though?'

'Why not? Drexler had made him look like an idiot. That's what he set out to do. He was successful. Drexler might even have given the money back voluntarily—that'd make him look generous to the girl, you see—and Mallory would look all the worse.' Sam picked a splay-shanked cold cigar out of an ash-tray, dusted it and re-lit it. 'Anyway you look at it, Paul, Drexler showed the girl he was much better qualified to advise her than the ex-boy friend. Mallory's stock would dwindle, Drexler's go up—and there you have it. But where's the connection between these people and Herb Rasch?'

127

'It's involved, Sam. I'll explain it when I've got more time.' Paul stood up. 'There are a lot of ways you can figure this case.'

'I believe that. The more I think about it the more I think Drexler knew his woman. A man'd hold him in contempt for giving the money back if he was threatened; that's the way I first looked at it, but now, well, I think he was smarter than I am; he knew by giving it back the girl would respect his judgment and concede his generosity. Clever; real clever, Paul.'

'So clever he forgot to make a study of Mallory—overlooked the thing that would kill him, and paid for it. See you again, Sam.'

The afternoon drew out. He didn't want to go back upstairs for fear Captain Benton would assign him to the dragnet for Rasch's killer. He ate an early dinner and cruised out past Golda's place in his personal car, circled the block and studied the neighbourhood. It was too early to risk crossing the backyards to Mike's place of vigil yet, but as soon as dusk descended he left the car, prayed the neighbours did not keep watchdogs and attempted it. Luck was with him. He made his way stealthily through a veritable forest of hedges, flowers and lawns, and found Mike watching his approach from behind the rose arbour.

'I'm hungry enough to eat a bear,' Mike said. 'You took her out and bought her

128

breakfast, didn't you? Didn't have any money and she had to write a cheque to pay for it.' Mike sniffed. 'That was clever; you wanted her signature or the name of her bank.'

'Name of her bank. How'd you know; did she call him?'

'As soon as you brought her back and left.' Paul looked at him steadily and Mike had a saturnine expression. 'There were other calls but not important ones. Just one other good one. Someone named Lugo called Golda's place for Mallory, when she told him she had no idea where he was this Lugo said for her to tell Mallory to carry a blank habeas corpus writ around with him, the cops were breathing down his neck.'

'Lugo?' Paul said blankly. 'There's no Lugo involved that I know of, Mike.'

'I know. It had me going for a while, too. I had lots of time to think out here. Maybe this Lugo's someone Bob Levin's after.'

'Check on it when you get back and I'll see you in the morning.'

'You going to stay on this thing all night?' Mike asked quizzically. 'Hell; she'll go to bed about twelve. There wouldn't be much doing after that, would there?'

'Probably not, but I want to be sure. If we muffed a lead now it'd be more than just embarrassing.' Mike left and Paul groped for the earphone, tested it and put it back under the loveseat. A long way off a dog barked, still farther out the low pulse of the city sounded soft. Overhead was a deep blue and inverted bowl with a tired half-moon surrounded by her raffish star-youngsters. Closer was the strong night-scent of flowers and because he couldn't smoke he wanted to.

The earphone clicked at his feet, he picked it up and placed it gently beside his head. A bell sounded twice then a voice he recognised came down the wire.

'Hello?'

'Pat, Golda. Any callers lately?'

'No, why?'

'I just wondered.'

Paul thought her voice sounded edgy, put it down to wishful thinking and pressed the earphone closer.

'Pat, I went out a little while ago and I think I was followed.'

Mallory was silent a second then, 'Followed? Why would anyone follow you? You must have imagined it.'

'Maybe, Pat—I'm nervous.'

'That's natural Golda, but you haven't done anything—why would anyone follow you.' There was a brief interval of silence then Mallory said, 'What did the man look like?' Paul detected a noticeable change in Mallory's tone. It was as though he was suddenly interested but making an effort not to be.

'It was too dark to see, Pat. Shorter than you are, possibly. Dark and swarthy perhaps—

130

thickly built in the body.'

Mallory cleared his throat. 'You must have imagined he was following you,' he said again, then fell silent.

Paul strove to remember Clampetti's description from the rap-sheet. Part of Golda's elaboration fitted but not all; for one thing Clampetti was taller—at least as tall as Mallory was. He squirmed on the loveseat. Could it have been this Lugo Mike had mentioned, and if so where did he fit in? Paul particularly did not want anything to happen to Golda; aside from her value, and Mallory's also for that matter. He had a private feeling for Golda; he couldn't have defined it if his life had depended upon it, but it was there nevertheless.

'That policeman last night, Pat,' Golda said abruptly. 'The one in the papers. That was terrible.'

'Why single out one detective to worry about,' Mallory said. 'A great many people are shot every year, Golda.'

'But you know what I mean.'

Mallory spoke swiftly, almost harshly. 'No I don't and you shouldn't think like that. I'll come over after breakfast in the morning.' He hung up, the line hummed in Paul's ear and he put the earphone in his lap. '. . . you know what I mean.' What did Mallory know—what did Golda mean? He bent, replaced the earphone and straightened up, twisted around

131

so that he could see the lights in her apartment through the fretwork of vines. He felt heavy inside. She was involved, he was certain of that. How deeply involved time would tell, but regardless, she was involved in a murder—possibly in more than just a murder—and that was inescapable. He ignored the caution of his own sixth sense, lit a cigarette behind cupped fingers, and smoked. Later, when the glow was short he put the thing out, stood up full height and stretched and looked at his wristwatch. The night was half gone, the neighbourhood was dark, only Golda's rear windows showed light. While he watched, her rooms darkened. He remained standing for a while, then began moving away, towards the hedge separating two rear yards. Passed through with some effort and walked out on to the sidewalk beyond, turned southward and strode towards his car.

For a while he did not drive away. Who was Lugo? A client of Mallory's? He'd check it out later. The engine spun to life and he drove slowly homeward. Each piece of the puzzle fitted into place except the key piece—linking Mallory to Drexler's murder. He swerved at the last moment and went to headquarters, walked to the communications room and asked if the tail he'd asked Captain Benton to put on Mallory's house had phoned in. He had not. Next, he called Benton at his home and inquired whether Benton had put a tail on

Golda Madison. Benton denied it but said he thought it was a good idea and where had Paul been all day and when was he going to make an arrest? He got rid of the captain as quickly as he could, went back out to his car, drove home and went to bed.

The second morning after Herb Rasch's killing the newspapers were beginning to hint at some dark collusion between the underworld and the department. Paul read them at his desk and pushed them aside angrily when Mike came in.

'Hear anything worthwhile?'

'Just some conversation, Mike. Tell me something—did she sound nervous to you yesterday?'

Mike shrugged. 'I don't know her well enough to know how she'd sound unnervous.'

Paul drummed on the desk. 'Well, she was nervous last night. She told Mallory someone was tailing her. He said it was her imagination—but she made one crack that interested me. She said Mallory would know what she meant about being nervous.'

Mike blinked and his brows drew down. 'She knows something? Something Mallory also knows—and we'd like to know?'

'I think that's it all right. Nothing turned up on Sabellis's employees?'

'Not a thing.' Mike rammed his hands deep into his trouser pockets. 'Cap'll be in here screaming like a wounded eagle any minute

133

now. Suppose I go sweat them out on the bug for a while.'

'No; go find out who Lugo is. By the way—'

'It's there under those other papers. The list of Mallory's clients. I can tell you from memory there's no Lugo there, too.'

The door swung inward, bounced off the wall and swung half closed after Bob Levin came in. He gave it a shove. 'The dragnet's a fizzle. What d'you think of that?'

Paul was gentle. 'You expected that, Bob. They usually are.'

'But I want this guy—I want him bad.'

'We understand.'

'I still think Lugo Sabellis could tell us something if he'd talk.'

Paul came slowly erect in his chair and Mike Karger turned fully to face Levin. 'Who?' he said. '*Lugo* Sabellis?'

'The guy at the Aloha.' Levin looked at them, moving his eyes slowly back and forth. 'What's the matter?'

'Nothing; nothing at all,' Mike said. 'Paul; I didn't run a make on *him*, remember? Going to and never got around to it.'

'He took us in, Mike. Okay, but hurry up. Bob and I'll wait right here.'

After Mike left, almost trotting, Bob Levin screwed up his face. 'What *is* this?' he demanded.

'We've got a lead on someone named Lugo who contacted Mallory and said the cops are

134

watching him, which isn't true so far as we know, but—'

'Like hell it isn't true,' Bob Levin said. 'I had a tail put on Lugo and of course the muttonhead let himself get seen.' Levin cracked his knuckles with a grim smile. 'That's probably what he meant about the cops watching him.'

'What have you got to go on?'

'Well; actually nothing, Paul, except that Clampetti was in his place before the shooting. It isn't very much but it's enough for a starter. Like I said—I want Clampetti bad.'

Mike came bounding back into the office a little breathless from taking the stairs two at a time. 'Brother,' he said explosively, 'did we almost make the mistake of our sweet lives. Here,' he put a stapled sheaf of papers on Paul's desk. 'Read that.'

Lugo Sabellis had served time at Elmire Reformatory at eighteen. At twenty he was arrested on a felony complaint. At twenty-three another felony count—both car thefts. At twenty-eight armed robbery for which he served seven years, time off for good behaviour. At thirty-seven he was arraigned for extortion but was acquitted. Paul glanced through the second page and dropped the report.

'He sure roped us in, Mike. Well—'

The telephone rang. It was Golda Madison, she wanted to know if Paul could drop by for a few minutes. There was a tightness to her tone that interested him. He agreed to meet her at the apartment within the hour and hung up. He was looking pleased.

'I think we're about to get a statement from Golda Madison. Mike; suppose you and Bob go out and call on Sabellis—take this rap-sheet . . .'

Mike smiled and reached for his hat. 'A pleasure,' he said. 'How about it, Bob?'

'Likewise. That was the Madison woman?' Paul nodded. 'Okay—I hope we turn up something. Benton's breathing fire. He said he had just one more day—today.'

Paul got up with a grimace. He said nothing, crossed to the door and and spoke from the opening. 'Let's try and meet here about noon or shortly thereafter. About Sabellis—use your judgment; if he looks like a good pinch bring him in, otherwise just put the fear of God into him. What I'm afraid of is that he's Mallory's pipe to Clampetti; if you guys find out that he is, then arrest him on anything you can come up with because what happens next depends on the hope we have that Clampetti doesn't actually contact Mallory.'

'I don't get it,' Levin said.

'Mike'll explain; we want Mallory to believe Clampetti's out to kill him. If Sabellis is Mallory's underworld contact he could upset the works; tip Mallory off Campetti isn't after him.'

'Well hell,' Mike said disprovingly, 'I think we'd better bring him in, Paul. There isn't much doubt now that he's Mallory's pipe.'

Paul shrugged. 'It's up to you fellows. I'll see you later.'

He arrived before Golda's apartment when the sun was slanting upwards towards the meridian, crushing the city under a pale, brassy blanket of muggy heat. To his surprise Pat Mallory met him at the door. They exchanged greetings. Golda swept into the room with a grave smile and asked if he'd like a cup of coffee. He agreed and so did Mallory. She started towards the kitchen and Paul watched her go. He sat upon the divan and Patrick Mallory dropped down in the chair across from him.

'What kind of red-tape do I have to go through to get a weapon's permit, Brewster?'

Paul swung his gaze. 'Concealed weapon?'

'Yes.'

'Show good cause first,' he replied, watching Mallory with interest, trying to probe behind the mask of his face. 'A clean record second; that's about all. Why do you want to carry a gun?'

'Well,' Mallory said evenly, 'after my car was stolen . . .' He looked up and Paul thought his expression was uneasy.

'That's not good enough cause. A hundred people have their cars stolen a day. If every one of them got a concealed weapon permit the city'd be like one of those old-time Western towns.'

'How about self-protection then?'

Paul nodded shortly. 'That's the best reason, but you'll have to explain it and what would a man in your position have to protect himself against?'

Mallory looked nettled. 'You had a detective killed the other night, cars are being stolen every day, it seems to me a citizen ought to be in a position to protect himself. Look what happened to Drexler.'

'If Drexler'd had a gun on his belt when he opened that door he wouldn't have had a chance to get it. He didn't know what was coming. You'd be in the same boat if someone wanted to blast you, Mallory, unless you knew in advance they might want to.'

Mallory gazed at the rug when he replied. 'Perhaps, but there's satisfaction in knowing you aren't entirely helpless.'

'Look,' Paul said leaning forward. 'If you've got a reason to think someone might be after you—some client you didn't get off the hook—something like that, why don't you let the police do the job for you? We can pick him up before anything happens. Afterwards it'd be too late to help you.'

Golda returned with a coffee tray, three cups and some silverware. Paul thought she was avoiding his gaze. He also felt that for the first time since he'd known Mallory, he, not the attorney, had the initiative.

'Have you found the man who killed that detective?' Golda asked.

'Not yet,' Paul said, and added nothing to it. There was a crackling moment of silence, then Mallory spoke.

'What about the Drexler case; anything new on that?'

'Nothing.'

The silence settled again, drew out thin. Golda folded a leg under her and concentrated on the coffee. Finally she asked Mallory if he'd care for another cup. He didn't reply, just held the cup out. Paul declined, lit a cigarette, laid the packet on a coffee table and leaned back to study Golda's face. It was clear now that she was avoiding his eyes.

'Did you have something in particular you wanted to see me about?' he asked her.

'Well; Pat and I'd been discussing Hugo's killing, and other things. We wondered if you'd come across anything. Our interest is personal, you know.'

'Sure,' Paul said, glancing at his wristwatch. 'I wish I had something for you. The fact is, Drexler's murder is a puzzler. I can't find a solid motive for it.'

'You said he was the witness to Kapelli's killing,' Mallory said.

'No; I said I *thought* he was; actually I don't know that he was.'

Mallory set his cup down and made a short,

explosive sound. 'Good God, Brewster; out at the ruin you told me Hugo probably was killed because he'd identified the gunman.'

Paul shook his head. 'Probably,' he said. 'I didn't say Drexler *was* the witness because I don't know that he was.'

'What kind of double talk is that?' Mallory demanded.

Paul got up, stooped for his hat and smiled at Golda. 'Mallory; these things take time. We're working on the Drexler case. You know better than I do that it takes more than a murder to get a conviction; we've got to have motive—intent. Thanks for the coffee. I've got a lot to do today so I'll say goodbye.'

Golda went to the door with him. Over her shoulder he could see Mallory's broad shoulders. He smiled down into her face and left.

The heat was more oppressive as the day wore on. He drove to a pay-station, mopped his face and put in a direct call to Captain Benton.

'This is Paul Brewster.'

'Where the hell *are* you? I've been—'

'Look, Cap, if Attorney Patrick Mallory comes down for a concealed weapon's permit today, refuse him.'

'Mallory? On what grounds?'

'Any grounds. We're out of forms, he'll have to file particulars, anything at all.'

Benton's voice dropped, got conspiratorial.

'Okay; I'll issue orders. What's up?'

'I just visited with Golda Madison and Mallory. They're afraid of something. I believe word has gotten back that Clampetti's out to kill him. Last night she told Mallory someone was tailing her.'

'A department man?'

'No; at least I didn't request it.'

'Neither did I,' Benton said. 'Look; just in case someone *is* out to get him—or her—I'd better put a couple of guards out there, hadn't I?'

'I think so, yes.'

'How about Mallory?'

'He's got a tail already.'

'Okay; I'll pass the word he's to be protected as well. Shouldn't we pick up these other tails?'

'Yes.'

Benton sighed. 'Is it stacking up the way we want it to?'

'I'm sure it is, Cap.'

'How much longer?'

'A matter of a few hours; at the most another day. As soon as Golda Madison's scairt enough to talk—or Mallory, although I'm not too hopeful there—we'll have him.'

'Good. Keep me posted, Paul, the Commissioner's riding me like a damned horse.'

'I will. Have Bob or Mike come in yet?'

'Not that I know of—no.'

141

'Okay; I know where they are, I'll contact them there.'

He hung up feeling good. Beyond the telephone kiosk was a drugstore with a gleaming counter. He entered, sucked in a big breath of the air-conditioned air and ordered a large dish of ice-cream, ate it slowly then went back to his car and drove out to the Miracle Mile, down the hill to the Aloha, parked and entered.

The place was like a tomb. Traffic hurrying by outside made a soft humming sound. He looked around the bar, saw no one, crossed through the dining-room which was also vacant, stopped on the opposite side of the room when he heard voices. One he recognised instantly as Mike Karger's. He knocked softly on the door with the gold star in the centre of it.

CHAPTER FIVE

When Paul entered Mike looked him squarely in the eye and nodded towards two handsome valises against the wall. While Bob Levin talked to Sabellis beyond earshot Mike said, 'That's how close we were to missing him. He was taking a powder, but good. There's fifty thousand dollars cash in one of those bags.'

Paul saw Sabellis's sweat-shiny face, flushed

now and agitated. He went to a chair without speaking and sat down. Mike Karger remained by the door. He looked enormous in a black suit, standing there against the cream coloured wall. Like a statue; an unpleasant statue.

Bob Levin's eyes were icy, his voice high and sharp. 'You lied about your background,' he was saying, 'and you lied about Clampetti. I already told you you're an accessory to murder. You set a man up for a murderer; don't tell me you didn't know Rasch.'

'I've put up with all this I have to,' Sabellis said, letting his eyes slide over Paul and back to Levin. 'I've got a right to call my attorney.'

'Sabellis,' Paul said quietly. 'What were you trying to do—gain time?'

Sabellis didn't answer right away. He let his breath out gently. Mike and Bob Levin watched him unblinkingly. 'I was only trying to protect my business,' he said.

'All right,' Paul said in the same tone. 'Maybe you were; I wouldn't blame you for that, you seem to have good trade, but why didn't you tell me last night about your record?'

'Why? Why?' Sabellis gestured with his hands. 'I didn't want to think about what would happen if you knew, I suppose. Look, officer, I've been bad. I've made plenty of mistakes—'but I swear to you I knew nothing about this murder, about those men.'

'You didn't know Rasch was a policeman—

143

that he was outside your nightclub watching it? You didn't know Clampetti—tell him there was a detective outside?'

'I swear it,' Sabellis said.

Paul gazed at the stocky nightclub owner. 'Then how did Clampetti know Rasch was outside—how did he happen to be here?'

'I give you my word I have no idea.'

'We knew he was here an hour before the killing. You had plenty of time to know it also.'

Sabellis leaned on his desk. His face was deathly pale. 'But I didn't *know* the man, I tell you. Sure; he could have been here all evening; I still didn't know him.' The black eyes were haggard. 'Are you going to take me in?'

Paul ignored the question. 'Someone in this neighbourhood was sheltering Clampetti—he was wanted for questioning about two other murders. Sabellis, murder is no joke. A cop-killer is no one to have anything to do with. No jury in this city'll give you any kind of a break with your past record.'

Sabellis's words spurted out. 'I am innocent; I don't own a gun; I don't know those kinds of people. Look; that man over there has my record—I ask you to look at it—I ask you to see when the last time I was in trouble. A number of years ago.' He waved around the room. 'I wasn't lying when I said I am respectable. I'm not a young man any more, officer, I've got a family—a good family—I know the difference between right and wrong.

144

It took me most of my early years to find that out but I found it out and I paid for finding it out. I can't say any more to convince you . . .'

Paul nodded towards the packed bags. 'What about those?'

'Yes,' Sabellis said with a quick, agitated nod. 'I was going to leave. I'll tell you why; I know how the police work; I knew they would do everything they could to nail me to a cross for my old record. It would break me fighting it—it would kill my family to know how I used to be.'

'And you also knew Clampetti might kill again—this time, you. You knew how deeply you were involved in something you can't buy or talk your way out of, Sabellis, so you thought the best thing you could do was run out.'

'That too,' Sabellis said, 'yes. A murderer doesn't reason. I was desperate, officer. I make no secret of that. I still am desperate.' He flashed glances at Levin and Karger. 'Ask these men—did I deny I was going away?'

Mike said, 'It's lucky for you, you didn't try it. That would have cinched you. Illegal flight to avoid prosecution.'

'If you want to call your attorney,' Paul said, arising, 'go ahead. The facilities where you're going aren't too good.' He crossed to Mike's side and spoke in a low tone. 'I hate to say this, Mike, because it's going to ruin our theory—but I believe him.'

145

'You're nuts,' Mike growled. 'He's as guilty as the devil himself.'

Paul turned back. Sabellis had one hand lying across the telephone on his desk, but he made no attempt to lift it. His gaze was fixed on Paul Brewster. He looked stricken.

'Sabellis,' Paul said softly. 'I can show enough evidence to book you as an accessory to murder. Go ahead and call your attorney.'

'How? Let me ask how?'

Paul nodded at the telephone. 'Call him.'

Sabellis was perplexed. After a time he took his hand off the instrument and glanced at it. 'Why do you want me to do that?'

'You said you had the right; I want you to exercise it.'

Bob Levin looked triumphant all of a sudden. Mike Karger still didn't comprehend, but just before Sabellis spoke again his eyes brightened.

'Go on, Sabellis, call him. Call Patrick Mallory!'

The black eyes lost their veil. 'I understand,' Sabellis said. 'You want to verify what you know about me.'

'That's right, but we want to verify a little more, too. We want to verify that you knew the police were watching you; that you wanted Mallory to be ready to spring you if you were arrested.'

'I'll verify that for you, sure. I called him after the killing out front last night. He knows

146

about my past.'

'And he knows more,' Paul said. *'He knew Anthony Clampetti killed Detective Rasch before the newspapers knew it!'*

'Mallory? How would he know that unless the police told him? I don't understand what you mean.'

Bob Levin got up suddenly. 'Let's finish with him downtown,' he said. 'Get your hat, Sabellis; let's go.'

They returned in two cars, Mike and Paul following Bob and Lugo Sabellis. Mike's broad face was dour. 'What the hell's got into you,' he asked Paul. 'That monkey's got enough against him to fry—almost.'

'I can't explain a hunch any more than you can, but I've got one—a strong one, Mike. I want you to do something for me.'

'What?'

'When we get back take my car, drive past Mallory's house and fire a couple of shots into it—up high.'

Karger looked stunned. 'Are you crazy?' he demanded. 'That wire-tap was risky enough. What the hell's the idea?'

'I want Mallory to know we've picked Sabellis up. The first thing he'll do after he thinks Clampetti's moving in for the kill, is try to contact Sabellis. When he can't he'll guess what's happened—that we have his contact man, *if* Sabellis *is* his contact man—and that'll settle the question in my mind about Sabellis's guilt or innocence; another thing, I'll have a plainclothes-man at the Aloha to take Sabellis's calls.'

'For God's sake, Paul,' Mike said in loud protest, 'we don't have to do anything as crazy as this—'

'It isn't just to verify the hunch about Sabellis. It's also to put the fear of God into Mallory. I want him to be so scairt he'll ask for police protection; I want him on the verge of believing the only way he can protect himself is to come to us.'

Mike stormed and swore all the way back to head-quarters but ultimately, as Paul knew he would, he agreed. They parted out front of headquarters. Paul followed Levin and Sabellis through the vestibule and down the first-floor corridor to Levin's office. Levin indicated a chair with a thumb, Sabellis dropped upon it gratefully. His shirt-front was damp and dark. He seemed numb, there was no expression on his face and only slightly more in his eyes. He watched Paul light a cigarette. When the packet was held out toward him he stared at it, then up at the tanned face above and shook his head.

'How long have you known Patrick Mallory, Sabellis?'

'Six, seven years. Since I bought the Aloha. He was my attorney during the deal.'

'How many times have you used his legal services?'

148

'A few times; when I bought an apartment house; once when I was sued—a woman fell at the club. The last time was about a year ago. I had an auto accident.'

'Did you know a man named Drexler; Hugo Drexler?'

Sabellis squinted in recollection and slowly shook his head. 'I don't think so; I meet a lot of people. Maybe I met him once or twice but I don't remember the name at all.'

'Did Mallory ever visit the nightclub?'

'Yes, once in a while, but it's been several months since I've seen him.'

'With a woman?'

'Different women, yes. He liked the ladies.'

Bob Levin tapped his desktop with a pencil. The sound became irritating but he made no effort to stop it. Twice Sabellis glanced significantly at the pencil. Levin's eyes never moved from his face and the pencil went on tapping. An hour or so later Levin's phone shrilled. He picked it up, spoke his name and held it out to Paul.

'This is Mike,' there was an electric undercurrent to the words. 'Listen; I played it smart for once. Right after I did what you wanted at Mallory's I beat it over to Golda's and listened in on the bug. He called her.'

'Upset?'

'Like the priest in a convent,' Mike said. 'But he didn't tell her why; asked if she'd seen anyone around her place; if anyone'd called

149

there asking for him. When she asked what was the matter he said nothing and hung up. I'll bet a month's pay she's ready to blow her top. This would be a good time to pick her up.'

'Not yet, Mike. Go back and watch that Mallory doesn't try to make a break for it.'

Mike hesitated. 'Paul,' he said finally, 'she's had it.' Mike went on but Paul's attention was distracted by the flashing light at the base of Levin's telephone. There was another call waiting on the line. He cut Mike short and pushed the button.

'Levin's office—homicide.'

'I'm trying to locate Detective Paul Brewster.'

He recognised the voice and his throat tightened. 'This is Brewster speaking.'

'Brewster, this is Patrick Mallory. Someone just tried to kill me. Fired two shots into my house, one went through the study wall and the other one broke two windows in my bedroom.'

Paul let a moment of silence go past. 'All right,' he said, 'now look, Mallory, why don't you tell me what this is all about?'

'I don't know. I want police protection out here.'

'You know all right. You knew something like this was going to happen when you wanted that concealed weapon permit. We're not putting any men out there to be targets until we know what we're up against. Now, if you

150

want that permit come on down and I'll see that you get it.'

'I'm not going to leave this house until I have protection. If you people won't provide it believe me I can get it from the District Attorney's office.'

'Okay,' Paul said placidly. 'Call them. I'll be out to see you in an hour or so.' He hung up. Bob Levin was watching him. Lugo Sabellis's face reflected wonderment. He flicked for an outside line, dialled the Aloha and got Sabellis's office. The voice was unfamiliar. He identified himself and asked who the other person was.

'Chuck Parker; Mike Karger called me to take calls.'

'Good; have there been any?'

'Just one. Some bird who wouldn't say who he was called for a bartender named Marty.'

Paul thanked the stake-out and turned to Sabellis. 'Who's Marty?'

'Marty? At my place? That'd be Marty Nichols the day-shift bartender.' Sabellis bit the last word off, stiffened in the chair. Paul noticed.

'What is it, Sabellis? What about this Marty Nichols?'

'I forgot.' The black eyes swivelled, landed on Paul's face and stayed there. 'Mallory recommended him to me.'

Paul turned to Levin. 'That's your baby, Bob,' he said rapidly. 'I think you're going to have to move fast. He's Mallory's pipe sure as hell. Mike looked up all Sabellis's employees last night but he's got the list with him. Get Nichols' address from Records, put out a call to pick him up then go down yourself and bring him in. Tell the arresting squad not to let him get near a telephone.'

Levin went out of the office without another glance at Lugo Sabellis and Paul dropped into his vacated chair. 'Sabellis, for your sake I hope this hunch is right. Tell me about Nichols.'

'He's a bartender, a fair one. He's steady, doesn't drink, doesn't say much, the customers like him. I've never had any complaints about him. Been with me about six months now.'

'Did you ever talk to him about Mallory?'

'Well, at first; only to make conversation. He told me he'd known Mallory about five years.' Sabellis asked for a cigarette. Paul gave him one and held the match. 'He didn't write on his employment blank that he'd ever been in trouble.'

'Apparently he hasn't. We checked out your people; the only one we found had a record was you.'

The black eyes flicked at Paul and away. Sabellis started to say something then changed his mind. Paul picked up the telephone, called for an officer from registration and hung up. 'You're going to be booked,' he said to Sabellis.

'The newspapers will have it, won't they?'

Paul stood up frowning. 'I could take a chance on you,' he said. 'I could hold you incommunicado, or upon your own recognisance. That way you wouldn't be booked and the reporters wouldn't get it off the blotter. But you'd have to request it, and you'd have to promise me not to call anyone from here.'

'I'll promise that,' Sabellis said. 'How long will I be here?'

'If you're on the up and up, not long. If you've lied again . . .'

'I haven't.' He stood up when the man in uniform entered. 'I want to say that I trust you.'

Paul said 'Protective custody,' to the officer from registration and affected not to hear what Sabellis had said. He remained standing in thought for several minutes after Sabellis had gone. A glance at his wrist-watch just as the phone on Levin's desk went off, showed him it was much later than he had thought; in fact it was early evening and he hadn't eaten since breakfast.

'Paul?'

'Yes; that you Bob?'

'It's me. Look; Nichols is holed up at one-twenty Main Street. It's a rooming house.' The door behind Paul opened, he twisted around and looked up. It was Mike Karger looking wilted but happy.

153

'I got it,' Paul said. 'One-twenty Main. You want us down there?'

'Yes. The squad men went up but he refused to open up to them. I got here about then and told them to hold off on forcing the door until I'd called you.' Levin paused then said, 'It looks like we might have a hassle down here.'

'Mike and I'll be right down. Don't let him slip out the back way, Bob.' He hung up and looked at Mike. 'Bob's got Sabellis's bartender holed up. Fellow named Marty Nichols; Mallory recommended him to Sabellis for a bartender.'

'What about him?'

'Someone called the Aloha asking for him. I've got a feeling it was Mallory. If it was, Nichols not Sabellis might be Mallory's underworld tap.'

'Well, I'm ready,' Mike said.

It was dusk when Mike wheeled his car beyond the maze of the city where housing developments in search of fresh air and sunlight had spread northeasterly toward the foothills. The houses were inexpensively built and almost before each neighbourhood was completed an appearance of dreariness settled over them. There was refuse, papers and beer cans in the gutters. Children played among the earthen scars left unhealed after the passage of giant earth-moving machines, dogs trotted through the byways and old automobiles sagged by the houses. Slatternly people moved or sat, as the spirit moved them, some glanced blankly at the black-and-white police sedan as it swung past.

One-twenty was an older house, two-storied, and had evidently been there years before the newer, smaller structures had been thrown up. Its exterior was cracked and unclean appearing. The windows were dry eyes made old with a knowledge of broken promises, stomped hopes and warped lives. There was an aloofness to the old building as though the crowding of newer homes was unnoticed in its sad vigil.

Mike cruised past, eased in at the kerb down the block from a squad car and a plain dark sedan, stopped and climbed out. He wrinkled his nose at the odours which came to him and walked around to the sidewalk where Paul was waiting.

'Want me to go around the back?' he asked.

Paul shook his head without answering. A uniformed man was standing by the front door looking down towards them. 'Let's talk to Bob first.'

Levin was smoking, leaning through the door of his dark sedan talking over the two-way. He called a 'ten-forty' when he saw them come up, hooked the microphone on its hanger and turned around.

'I went in and talked to him after I called in. He says we'll have to produce a warrant before he'll let us in or come out and talk to us.'

Mike looked up at the old wreck of a building. 'What's he scairt about?' he asked.

Levin shrugged. 'Who knows? A guilty conscience'll push a guy right into trouble when there isn't any around except what he makes himself.'

Paul unbuttoned his coat, put his hand under it and pulled the hold-down loose on his holster. Without looking at either of his companions he said, 'When I was at the police academy they used to say a good cop doesn't use his gun—he uses his prestige. I guess I'm not a good cop. Bob; who's around in back?'

'One of the harness bulls. They put in a call for reinforcements. They ought to show up any moment if you want to wait.'

'I'll go up and have a talk with him,' Paul said. 'Which roach-trap is his?'

'Go upstairs and turn right. His door is the second one down. Be careful, Paul; when I called to him to come out he sounded like he meant what he said.'

'Let's wait,' Mike said.

'Can't,' Paul said shortly. 'I want this bird alive. If he gets troublesome around these squad men I know what'll happen.' He walked away from them. The uniformed officer at the door blocked his path. A show of identification cleared the obstacle. The stair-well was darker than dusk. It had an unhealthy odour and each stair squeaked protest when he put his weight down on it. Upstairs he stopped to listen.

Somewhere a man was snoring liquidly, each exhalation accompanied with a strangling bubble of moisture. Probably drunk, Paul thought, and went towards the second door on the right. There wasn't a sound from behind it.

'Nichols!'

No answer; he raised his fist and rapped sharply. Echoes chased each other into oblivion down the dingy hallway.

'Nichols; open the door.'

'Who are you and what do you want?'

'I'm a police officer and I want to ask you a couple of questions. Open up.'

'You got a warrant?'

'I don't need a warrant to ask questions.'

'You need one to make me open that door.'

'Don't be a fool,' Paul said. 'I don't need any warrant to go through your door. All I've got to do is get the landlord's permission to kick it open—he's the owner, you're not.' It wasn't true but Paul hoped it sounded plausible. Nichols retreated into silence again. Paul waited, then decided to try once more.

'What're you hiding, Nichols? Look; I'm not going to play around here all day. Either you open the door right now or I'm going after the landlord. Make up your mind.'

The door swung inward. A tall, curly-headed man in his middle thirties stood wide-legged beyond the opening. His eyes were unfriendly but he had no gun in sight. Paul entered the room and was immediately

157

struck by a peculiarly sweet—and familiar—odour. He jerked a thumb toward the bed, there was only one chair in the room, over by the window; obviously it had been used by Nichols for his vigil.

'Sit down over there.' Nichols sat, his hands shook when he lit a cigarette and blew smoke straight out. Paul moved toward the window without turning his face away from Nichols. He caught Karger's and Levin's attention and beckoned.

'Heroin, Nichols?' he asked. 'How long have you been on the needle?'

'Tell you nothing,' Nichols said surlily, avoiding Paul's face.

'I don't care,' Paul said leaning over the back of the chair. 'It's your life you're ruining, not mine. I could show you junkies who've been on it longer than you have though—they'd turn your stomach.'

'Make your pinch and shut up.'

'I'll make it but first we're going to talk a little.'

'Tell you nothing,' Nichols said again.

Mike and Bob came through the door, looked at the man on the bed and stopped. Mike drew handcuffs from under his coat but made no move to use them. Levin sniffed, looked at Paul and on to Nichols, screwed up his nose and wagged his head.

Paul sat down in the chair. 'We're not here about the monkey on your back,' he said, and

Nichols looked up quickly, a short, probing glance. 'Weren't you supposed to be on duty at the Aloha this afternoon?'

'Got held up,' Nichols said.

'That's too bad. Pat Mallory called you there.'

Nichols' shoulders hunched perceptibly, he remained silent. A big uniformed man came quietly to the door and stopped. He almost completely filled the opening. Mike Karger threw the light switch and a solitary lamp near the bed glowed.

'Know why Mallory called, Nichols?' No reply. 'Because he wanted you to tell Clampetti he hadn't used him in the Drexler murder; not to believe the rumours that he had.' When Nichols still refused to be drawn out Paul arose and motioned to Mike. Nichols was handcuffed and pushed toward the door. The uniformed officer took him by the arm down the stairs and out on to the darkening sidewalk. Across the street a small, hushed assemblage of curious people stood motionless.

'I'll follow you, Bob,' Paul said. 'You and Mike take him in.' He moved towards the waiting squad-car men as Nichols was hustled into Levin's car. 'You fellows can get back on beat—thanks.'

At headquarters Marty Nichols remained stubbornly silent. Paul, Mike Karger, and Bob Levin hammered at him with questions. He

159

kept his eyes on the ground and would not be drawn out. In disgust Bob Levin pulled him out of the chair and out the door toward booking.

'Book him on suspicion?' he asked Paul over his shoulder.

'Make it better than that,' Paul replied. 'Make it accessory to murder.'

Nichols jerked free of Levin, swung and glared at Paul. 'Make it anything you want,' he said, 'you sonsofbitches!'

Levin gave him a rough push, they disappeared down the corridor. Mike puffed up his cheeks and blew out a big breath. 'He's really hot, isn't he?'

'Yeah. Mike, I've got to go out to Mallory's for a while. "You want to stay here or ride along?'

'I'll go along.'

When they got to Patrick Mallory's residence his man kept the front door on the chain until he was satisfied as to their identity. Mike shot Paul a look.

Mallory was in the panelled study with the blinds closed and the lights on. He did not appear outwardly to be as agitated as Paul had expected. After a brief greeting he pointed out a slivered gouge in the wall several inches higher than his head. Paul craned to peer at it and gazed sideways at Mike. Karger's face had paled.

'There's another one upstairs,' Mallory said

moving toward a dark leather chair. 'Did you bring the forms for the gun permit Brewster?'

'No; I wanted to talk to you first.'

Mallory's eyes flashed. 'Talk? What more do you need than those two bullet holes?'

'The name of the man who fired the shots.' Mallory's face darkened. 'Are you implying I *know?*' he demanded.

Paul shook his head. 'I'm implying you have an *idea* who he was.'

'Well, as usual,' Mallory said, 'the police deductive processes are wide of their mark.'

Paul stood gazing at Mallory. A moment later he turned with a shrug of defeat. 'All right, Mallory; we'll take you down to headquarters for the permit.' He glanced at his watch. 'I'd like to use your telephone to phone in, if you don't mind.'

Mallory arose, led them to the instrument and excused himself to get dressed for the street. When his footfalls had grown faint upstairs Paul turned to Mike Karger.

'He'll probably listen in on an upstairs phone. I'll go up and stay with him while he's dressing. You call Benton or Levin and have them take Nichols to Bob's office. Tell them we're bringing Mallory in for the pistol permit and that we'll take him down the hall past Bob's office. We want him to see them questioning Nichols. Okay?'

Mike nodded without speaking and Paul went up the stairs two at a time. From the landing he nodded at Mike then disappeared to the left.

Mallory may have had some idea of listening in for he was near the bedroom telephone stand when Paul walked in, but he also had fresh linen in one hand and a suit coat in the other. He looked a shade resentful at Paul.

'What's this—belated protection?'

'Call it that if you like.' Paul crossed to a chair near the darkened window and sat down, shoved his legs out and watched Mallory dress. 'I'd rather nothing happened to you while you're with us.'

When they went back downstairs moments later Mike was waiting by the front door, a thoughtful look on his face, his hat parked on the back of his head. He surveyed Mallory silently, opened the door and closed it afterwards. There was just enough moonlight to cast the weakest, wateriest of shadows. Mallory hesitated a moment, then walked hurriedly toward the car at the kerbing. Little was said en route. They purposefully entered the building by the small door opposite the identification bureau and started up the long corridor toward the front desk. Their steps echoed hollowly. One door stood wide open and a long slanting dagger of light made a patch across the hallway. Twenty feet from the opening Paul could hear Captain Benton's voice cutting at Nichols. Words seemed to hurtle into the stillness, explode in mid-air. He watched Mallory from the corner of his eye. Mike Karger walked stolidly on the other side of Mallory but just as they approached the door he lagged a few inches. Mallory had an unobstructed view. When he was abreast the opening he looked in. A momentarily visible reaction showed in his walk, a slight stiffening of the gait. Paul, looking beyond, saw Nichols' head raise, the dull eyes focus on the passing man, follow him with oily persistency for the flash of time required for Mallory to pass by and beyond, and he was satisfied. Also visible for that second was the pale face of Levin and the mottled, wrathy expression of Captain Benton.

Mallory said nothing until they were at the desk in the front office and Paul had asked for a concealed weapon permit application, then he turned, leaned on the counter while the desk officer went to a filing cabinet.

'Wasn't that Captain Benton?'

'Yes.'

'Who was the prisoner?'

Paul met his stare. 'Didn't you recognise him?' he asked evenly, and Mallory flushed.

'Why should I recognise him?'

'Oh; I thought he was a client of yours.'

'Of mine? Did he say that?'

'He said that before I went out to your place; I don't know what he's said since.'

Mallory let the application form lie

unnoticed after the officer brought it back. He was searching Paul Brewster's face. 'Look, Brewster,' he said finally in a cold voice. 'I'm familiar with police routine. Just exactly what are you trying to do?'

'Find a murderer, Mallory; that's what I've been after since the first day we met.'

'And now you'd like to implicate me, isn't that it?'

Paul touched the concealed weapon permit form, pushed it towards Mallory without looking at him. 'Here; fill this out and go on home. If I'd wanted to implicate you that alibi would have stopped me—it's too perfect.' He looked up into the acid features. 'I don't know all that's going on and maybe I never will—but I know this: If someone's out to kill you, and you won't come clean with us so we can protect you—he may succeed, in which case we'll probably never know, but you won't be the first unsolved case on our files, as you know. Go ahead, fill it out.'

Mallory made no move to reach for the form. 'Brewster, I want to warn you. The law is made to protect as well as to prosecute people.'

Mike Karger sighed and leaned heavily on the counter. 'Mr. Mallory,' he said, 'we know that better than you do.'

'I doubt it,' Mallory replied shortly. 'If you attempt to prosecute anyone you'd better be very certain of your grounds.'

164

'We're certain of that man Captain Benton was talking to,' Paul said. 'We know exactly who he is and what he did.'

'Did?'

'Yes, that's the man who fingered Detective Herb Rasch for Anthony Clampetti. We don't know yet how he knew Rasch on sight, but that's a small detail. Law-breakers, even minor ones without police records, have long memories for policemen. That man's name is Nichols, he's a bartender at Lugo Sabellis's nightclub the Aloha. He recognised Rasch and fingered him for the man who killed him.'

'He may have,' Mallory said. 'What of it? Killings like that aren't very involved. A man with a record and a grudge—'

'Nichols has no record. He's a narcotics addict but apparently hasn't been on the needle very long; not long enough to have caught the narcotics squad's attention.'

Mallory shrugged and looked down at the form. 'All right; record or no record, he had a grudge against Rasch.'

'It was better than that,' Paul said. 'Someone told him to watch out for cops while Clampetti—the man who murdered Hugo Drexler and Kapelli—was at the Aloha. He did; he recognised Rasch, and Clampetti killed him.'

Mallory picked up a pen and bent over the form. He spoke in a disinterested tone. 'All you have to do then is take him to court on an

165

accessory charge.'

'Sure, but he's going to tell us who told him to watch for cops.'

Mallory looked around with the pen poised. 'This Clampetti must have. That's obvious. Why would anyone else bother?'

'Because Clampetti is a lone-wolf torpedo, Mallory. We've got his record since his first arrest; he took money for the things he did but he aways operated alone and had no confidants.'

'So you suspect conspiracy,' Mallory bent again, began writing in a cramped, distinct hand.

'We *know* there was a conspiracy. All we want now is for Nichols to tell us who was behind it.'

Mallory wrote without speaking. Mike sought Paul's glance, caught it and raised his eyebrows. Paul ignored the movement, lit a cigarette and waited patiently until Mallory was finished, then he picked the form up and read it with his eyes pinched down against the upward sweep of smoke. He laid it on the counter, removed the cigarette and spoke.

'All right; I'll have it processed. The permit will be mailed to you.'

Mallory frowned. 'Why can't I get it right now?'

'You don't have the gun with you, do you?'

'No.'

'We'll want to register the serial number,

166

make and model.'

'That's easy. I have the gun registered here as belonging to me. You can get the information from your records.'

'We're required by city ordinance to inspect the gun for safeness, among other things.'

Mallory made a face. 'Redtape,' he said. 'How long will it take?'

'Half an hour, seldom longer.'

'All right; suppose I give you the gun when we get back to my house. You can bring it in yourself and notify me when the permit's ready.'

'That'll be all right,' Paul said. 'Come on; we'll take you home.'

Mike demurred. 'You won't need me,' he said. 'Suppose I help them sweat Nichols out?'

Mallory was looking down toward the square of light in front of Levin's office. 'I'd like to talk to that man,' he said to Paul. 'If he says I'm his attorney I'd like another look at him.'

'Let's wait until he calls you, Mallory. He was probably just talking. You know how those people are; they say anything that pops into their heads when they're in trouble.'

'Nevertheless, if he's a client I'd like to see him.'

Paul turned away. 'Come on,' he said.

They went to Levin's office. Captain Benton looked up as the three of them entered. Nichols was blank-faced, there was a rash of

167

perspiration across his upper lip, aside from that he looked as surly as he had from the first. Bob Levin shot a quick glance at Mallory, it was more curiosity than anything else. He was leaning on the wall smoking, now he pushed upright and let the cigarette hang from his fingers.

Mallory went over in front of Nichols. 'You don't have to tell the police anything,' he said in a matter-of-fact and dispassionate voice, 'until you've had legal advice.' Nichols looked up at him for a moment then his eyes slid past, rested on Paul Brewster's face. He said nothing.

'Do you know him, Mallory?'

The attorney frowned as though endeavouring to recollect. 'Possibly,' he said. 'I may have represented him some time. Right off hand I don't recall. Your name is Nichols? I understand you told the police I am your lawyer.' Nichols looked up swiftly, there was a perplexed, harassed expression on his face. Noticing, Mallory spoke swiftly. 'It doesn't matter; I take it you want me to represent you now. Good, the first thing I advise you to do, Mr. Nichols, is to say nothing. Absolutely nothing at all. I'll be around to see you again in the morning. Is that agreeable with you?'

Nichols finally spoke. 'Yeh,' he grunted.

Mallory looked over the prisoner's head, saw Captain Benton watching him and nodded. 'Good night,' he said, and turned toward Paul. 'Let's go.'

They drove Mallory home in silence. Mike went to the door, waited until Mallory returned with the gun, pocketed it and walked back to the car, got in and yawned. 'That was just about a total waste of time,' he said.

'Not altogether, Mike.'

'Mallory queered Nichols for us, you didn't plan that did you?'

'Let Nichols keep his mouth closed, who cares? What's important is that Mallory knows we've got him; he'll begin to sweat now.'

'You hope he does,' Mike said dourly.

'Look, Mike; Nichols was Mallory's contact man with Clampetti. With Nichols out of circulation there'll be no way for him to pass the word to Clampetti he is being duped by the police on the Drexler murder.'

Mike yawned again. 'All right,' he said. 'Let's knock off and get some sleep. I'm too tired to think any more today.'

'Just one more play, Mike. You can drop me off about a block from Madison's, drive uptown and call Golda. Make it mean—tell her if she knows what's good for her she'll get out of town. Tell her Patrick Mallory's pulled his last double-cross, then hang up.'

Mike nodded assent. 'All right; I get it.'

Paul got out of the car and waved Mike away when he was near Golda Madison's apartment building. He took his time about arriving at the door, rapped softly and glanced at his wristwatch. It was close to eleven o'clock. The knowledge made him yawn while he waited. When she opened the door it was on the nightlatch-chain. She peered out at him fully clothed, moved back and swung the door open. He stopped and waited while she re-locked it.

'Sorry to bother you when it's so late.'

'I was up reading anyway,' she said. 'Please sit down; can I make you a highball, Mr. Brewster?'

He sank down on the sofa. 'No thanks. I was passing by,' he said. 'Thought I'd drop in for a moment.'

She crossed a leg under her and leaned back in a chair across from him. 'You have awful hours, haven't you?'

'Sometimes; this time it was Mallory,' he said watching her.

'Pat? Has something happened?'

'No—at least not yet—he wanted a permit to carry a concealed weapon. That's why I thought I'd drop in and have a chat with you. Someone took two shots at him today. He wouldn't tell us anything about it and I thought you might be able to help us locate an enemy of his. Someone who hates him badly enough to pull a Drexler on him.'

She was white-faced and large-eyed. 'Not Pat,' she said in a strained way. Quite suddenly she arose, moved across the room to the sideboard and stood there a moment, then

170

mixed herself a drink and took it back to the chair and sat down. 'What could I tell you?'

'You could start at the beginning,' Paul said.

'What do you mean?'

Mindful that she would call Mallory as soon as he left, Paul lingered over the phrasing of his reply. 'For one thing—what are you afraid of Miss Madison?' He cut off the protest he saw forming with a gesture. 'I'd rather you didn't tell me anything if you don't intend to tell me the truth.'

She drank deeply, set the glass aside and stared at him in silence. Finally she lit a cigarette and blew the smoke outward. 'I've already told you everything I know about Hugo's murder.'

'Is it that simple?' he asked.

'Simple,' she said explosively, as though he'd touched a spring within her. 'It's anything but simple, Mr. Brewster.'

'What makes you say that?'

'Last night I had to go out. A man followed me.' She crushed the half-smoked cigarette. 'It wasn't imagination, I saw him.'

'I didn't say it was imagination, Miss Madison.'

'No, *you* didn't—I saw him quite plainly. He was a heavily built dark looking man.'

'Why would anyone follow you?'

'I have no idea.'

The telephone rang. She crossed to it, put it to her head and listened. He watched her

171

profile, saw the quick, spasmodic tightening of her features. She held the instrument out a second then replaced it as though in a trance.

'Anything wrong?'

'It was that man.'

'The one you say followed you?'

'Yes. I'm sure it was him. He warned me to leave the city.'

'Did he say anything else?'

She shook her head, remained where she was a moment longer then went back to the chair and sat down slowly. She did not face him and obviously she was badly frightened. He let her sit in silence for several minutes then got up.

'Miss Madison; when you're ready to tell me what this is all about call me.' He went to the door, threw off the chain and opened it. 'I could put a man here for protection if you'd feel better.'

She got up and crossed to the door, spoke without looking at him. 'I'll call you.'

He went down across the patio, but instead of going out to the sidewalk he cut swiftly to his right, hurried along the cement driveway to the rear yard, crossed its broad sweep of lawn to the arbour and groped frantically for the earphone.

'. . . Left just this minute, Pat.'

'You mean he was there when the man called?'

'Yes.'

172

'Did you tell him about the call?'

'All but that last part; when the man said you'd pulled your last double-cross. Pat; who is he? Isn't there some way you can make peace with him? I'm—'

'Be quiet and listen. I can't make peace because I don't know where he is any more. I had a friend of his I could contact him through but he's been picked up—a bartender I met in Reno two years ago.'

'What can you do?'

'I've got to find him, Golda, before he finds me,' Mallory said, and Paul heard the tension in the words. 'I'll do it—don't worry I'll find him.'

'How, Pat? I'm terribly frightened. Couldn't we—?'

'I'll hire some of the underworld characters I've represented to find him; I'll pay them well. It'll work out.'

'But what if they *don't* find him, Pat? Is he the one who shot at you? Oh, Pat . . .'

'Golda, stop it! Brewster has absolutely nothing—nothing at all. He can think what he wishes but he can prove nothing.'

'I'm afraid of him,' she said quickly. 'He's nowhere nearly as phlegmatic as you said he was.'

'I don't give a damn if he's Einstein,' Mallory swore, 'he can't prove anything against us as far as Drexler's death is concerned—absolutely nothing—so don't you

173

say anything to him about it at all. Refer him to me—tell him I'm your legal counsel and you won't discuss anything with him unless I'm present. Now remember that, Golda.'

'I'll remember, Pat, but I'm not as worried about him as I am about these other things. The shots at you, that man following me . . .'

'Get hold of yourself,' Mallory said. 'I'll see you tomorrow.' He hung up.

Paul sank down on the cold, iron loveseat and replaced the earphone, lit a cigarette with his back to the building and smoked it in the vague night-shadows. It wouldn't be long now; she was ready and Mallory—contrary to Paul's expectations—was almost as upset. Only one question bothered him. Had someone really followed her or was it imagination? He stood up and looked about. There was nothing but night, silence, and stillness, around him. He'd have another man or two stake-out the apartment house. And just in case Mallory's nerve broke he'd have orders passed to apprehend him the moment he left his building with a valise.

By the time he got to the telephone pay-station the night had grown crisp. He called for a taxi, waited it out in the shadows of a drugstore and was driven home savouring a feeling of elation over the nearness of triumph.

174

CHAPTER SIX

It was four a.m. when the telephone beside the bed went off with startling abruptness. Paul sprang up in bed with his heart thudding, groped for the lamp switch, flooded the bedroom with light and picked the instrument off the bedstand.

'Brewster here.'

'Benton. The lady's gone.'

'What!'

'She pulled it real cute, put on her maid's outfit and went out the back way. The stake-out saw her, assumed it was the maid and only called in because he thought it odd the maid was so late going home. We went out there—the place was as empty as a tomb.'

'Cleaned out?'

'No; it looks like about all she took was some clothes. She may have taken some money if she had some lying around the apartment, but everything else is there. I got two men at the apartment and another one outside.'

'How long ago?'

'Maybe an hour—maybe a little before.'

'You put out A.P.Bs?'

'Yes, and stake-outs at the train and 'plane depots—calls to the squad cars—everything I could do.'

Paul ran a hand through his hair and squinted at the far wall. 'How about the stake-out at Mallory's?'

'Nothing; he reported in a while back. Mallory's at home, the place is dark and no one's been casing it.' Captain Benton blew cigarette smoke into the mouth-piece, it made a hollow and surf-like roar. 'Where would she go and what scairt her badly enough to try it?'

'I think I scairt her that badly, only at the time I didn't think she'd do *this*.'

'Then you'd better get down here and undo it,' Benton said and hung up.

By the time he got downtown Mike Karger and Bob Levin were already there. Captain Benton was showing them on his chart how the city had been closed to Golda Madison. Paul looked as he went past to his desk. Someone had shown uncommon foresight; there was a pot of hot coffee and some heavy crockery cups on the desk. He poured and drank, made a face over the strength of the fluid and began shuffling through the pile of papers on his desk. Captain Benton turned to stare at him.

'What you doing?'

'Looking for a name among Mallory's cashed cheques.'

'Madison's?'

'No, Nichols. I've a notion Mallory must have paid Nichols to watch for Clampetti.' He continued to shuffle through the lists but finally gave it up. There were too many "cash" withdrawals with no notations of payees behind them. 'Okay; it was a fluke. Now what about Golda?'

'Don't ask me,' Benton said. 'I could shoot that stake-out.'

'Forget it,' Paul said, 'how could you expect him to know it wasn't the maid?'

Benton did not reply, but Mike Karger said, 'Mallory'll be next.'

That time Benton replied. 'Like hell he will,' he said. 'I got word to the stake-out at his place to pick up anyone at all who goes in or comes out no matter who they are.'

Paul sat down, picked up the telephone and got Mallory out of bed. 'Brewster. Miss Madison's disappeared, Mallory, I was wondering if you'd know where she could have gone?'

'Disappeared! What do you mean?'

'She left her apartment about three o'clock this morning dressed in her maid's get-up.'

Mallory swore and his voice became alive, vibrant sounding. 'She wouldn't do that voluntarily,' he said, then he was silent a few seconds. 'Maybe she would; she was afraid of something the last time I talked to her.'

'When was that?'

'Last night; about eleven-thirty I'd say.'

'Did she *say* she was afraid?'

'She told me some man had called her—told her to get out of the city.'

'Is that all?'

'Yes; as well as I can remember right now. I have no idea who her caller was nor why he'd threaten her, but obviously she decided to do as he'd said. Look, Brewster, if you find her have her call me immediately, will you?'

'Sure,' Paul said and hung up, sat at the desk looking at Mike. 'Let's take a ride over to her apartment, Mike.' When he stood up Captain Benton scowled unpleasantly.

'There's a stake-out there, I told you.'

'We'll send them back—maybe leave just the outside man.'

'What the hell can you accomplish there, I ask you!'

'I won't know until I'm there,' Paul retorted, putting his hat on, 'but there's nothing we can do sitting here, either.'

They sent back the two plainclothesmen at Golda Madison's apartment and were finishing a cursory examination of the premises when Patrick Mallory came through the unlocked door. Mike looked around surprised but Paul Brewster only nodded.

'Took you longer than I thought,' he said.

Mallory looked suspicious. 'What does that mean?'

'She was your girl-friend wasn't she? It'd only be natural for you to take an interest in her disappearance.'

'Everything you say seems to have a double meaning, Brewster. She was a friend, not a girl-friend, and you know it.'

Paul let it go by, watched Mallory prowl over the place. He and Mike were in the kitchen when they heard Mallory emit a sharp, high curse. Going to the girl's bedroom they watched him straighten up from behind the nightstand with a small, dull box in his palm. Paul went closer and peered.

'A bug,' he said. 'Was it tapped to her telephone?'

Mallory's gaze was speculative and suspicious. He nodded without answering. Paul looked into his eyes, read the expression and shook his head.

'Not me, Mallory. I didn't put it there. Look; you ought to be able to tell us something. Those shots at your house, some guy Miss Madison told me last night had been following her,' he bobbed his head at the listening device. 'A bug on her phone and her disappearance. Girl-friend or just friend, you've known her a long time; you'd have an inkling if she was in some kind of trouble, wouldn't you?'

Mallory dropped his glance to the bakelite box he held, turned it over in his hand and sank down on the edge of the bed. 'Who put this in here?' he asked blankly.

'Mallory—someone's in trouble to their armpits—serious trouble—forget the bug for the moment.'

'Trouble, yes,' Mallory said sharply. 'This is absolutely illegal.' He got off the bed. 'I'm going to trace-out the phone line. Wherever the earphones are . . .' He started off without finishing. Paul slid a surreptitious glance at Mike and turned to help move the furniture. It required nearly half an hour to find the line leading to the arbour and when Patrick Mallory picked the single earphone out of the grass he looked puzzled.

'Why here?'

'Where'd you expect it to lead,' Pat said, 'to some guy's house uptown?'

Mallory gazed at him in perplexity. 'Who would . . .? Do you suppose someone really was following her? I mean,' he gestured towards the comparative seclusion of the arbour, 'who would sit out here . . .?'

'It looks to me,' Paul said, 'as though someone was keeping an awfully close watch on her. But why?'

Mallory put the earphone on the loveseat and turned slowly to study the houses paling in false-dawn around them. He completed the circle and stared up at Golda Madison's apartment. 'I don't get it,' he said to himself. There was genuine uneasiness on his face; fear.

'Come clean,' Paul said.

Mallory turned and stared at him without speaking. Mike was struck by the grey colour of Mallory's face. 'Mr. Mallory,' he said, 'why don't you quit fooling around. Police protection isn't going to do you much good unless the police know what they're supposed to protect you against. If you won't help us we can't help you.'

Mallory turned and walked out of the arbour. They followed him back to Golda's apartment where he mixed himself a strong drink at the bar, drank it with his back to them, set the glass down and lit a cigarette. Colour returned to his face. 'I'm at a loss, completely at a loss.'

Paul believed him but didn't show it. 'You didn't advise her to run out, did you?'

'Why? What possible reason could I have for doing that?'

'I'm asking. You were her adviser; her financial adviser and for all we know her personal adviser. You were also at one time her fiancé.'

Mallory ran a hand over his cheek and Paul saw the bulge of a gun at his armpit. 'Of course I didn't advise her to do this; I'm not convinced she did it voluntarily, either.'

'What makes you say that? She was afraid of something—we all know that. She was warned over the phone last night to get out of town.'

'But—I talked to her last night, she didn't even mention such a thing.'

'Then for the time being we'll have to assume she ran out under her own free will.'

'No,' the attorney said. 'No, I don't believe that.' He crossed the room to the chair where his hat lay, picked it up and held it in his hand.

181

'Mallory,' Paul said, 'we've heard a pretty reliable rumour someone's out to kill you. We heard it even before you applied for the pistol permit.'

'Who is it?'

'We couldn't find out.'

'Who told you?'

'Your client Nichols.'

Mallory sank down on a sofa. 'I'll talk to him in the morning. He'll tell me.'

'Yes, I think he will, but even if he does it isn't going to help you very much.'

Mallory looked up. 'What do you mean?'

'If you know the killer how can you know when he's going to make his play? You can't— and that's where the fatality comes in.'

'I don't understand,' Mallory said again, but his voice lacked conviction.

'Whatever you know, Mallory, whatever you've done,' Paul said, 'certainly can't be the equivalent to a death sentence. Why don't you wise up and trade your knowledge for full police protection. If you don't this guy's going to kill you anyway.'

'I want a cordon of police around my house,' Mallory said, his voice gaining strength again. 'I'm entitled to that.'

'You've got it. Your place has had a stakeout on it for several days.'

Mallory looked incredulous. 'I don't believe it,' he said, 'I haven't seen any men around.'

'You won't see them but they're there just

'the same. Still, the bird who threw those shots at the house could get past. What good is the cordon if it doesn't know what to look for?'

'Anyone at all; have them arrest any one who looks suspicious. That's no problem.'

'Isn't it,' Paul retorted. 'How about the milkman, the grocer, the telephone serviceman, the laundryman—any one of them could be your killer.'

'Stop every one of them. Listen, Brewster, you people have arrested innocent men before on suspicion, you certainly can do it again—until—'

'And have a false-arrest suit brought against the city? Not on your life. The primary elections are only a few days off, Mallory. All the Commissioner'd need right now would be a police blunder and some derogatory publicity.'

'Commissioner be damned!' Mallory exploded. 'There's a life at stake.'

'Calm down,' Mike said. 'If you won't help us we can't help you. I already told you that. If you know who this guy is you'd better tell us. Your funeral won't make much of a ripple in the city.'

The telephone rang and Paul threw it an irate glance. The interruption at this point was unwelcome. Mike hooked it with taloned fingers and barked his name into the mouthpiece.

'Bob Levin, Mike. Nichols is throwing a fit

183

down in the tanks. He needs a fix. Cap and the department physician are in favour of giving him a jolt—I wanted them to hold off until I could contact you and Paul. My idea's to let him writhe for a while—until he'll tell us where Clampetti's holed up. What about it?'

Mike held the instrument toward Paul, who spoke his name, listened for a moment, then said, 'Good; fine. That's exactly the break we needed. Okay; we'll be right over.' When he hung up he had no way of knowing that Bob Levin was looking at the telephone as though he hadn't heard right, then he put it on its cradle and scratched his head.

'Mallory,' Paul said feigning triumph, 'we know where Drexler's killer is. When we get him we'll sweat it out of him who tipped him off about Rasch—who the finger was who told him about Drexler. He might even be the guy who's after you, what do you think?'

'I don't know; if there's a connection I can't see it.'

'Can't you? Well, we'll come around and see you later.'

When they were getting into the police sedan outside Mike asked where Clampetti was and Paul said he had no idea. Mike looked pained.

'What the hell was that back there—bluff?'

'Pure and simple,' Paul said. 'And when we get back I'm going to call Mallory and tell him Clampetti escaped us. I want him to really

184

sweat today.'

Mike waited until they had parked in front of headquarters before he said, 'Let's get some breakfast.'

They went across the street, had coffee and eggs, finished and went back outside. The sun was bursting upon a spire of the tallest downtown skyscraper. Molten heat was gushing like lava along the cement canyons. They crossed to the main entrance beyond their car, entered and went down the east corridor to Levin's office. He greeted them with a puzzled look.

'Say, what the hell; I tell you something over the phone and you act like it's Christmas.'

'Mallory was listening,' Paul replied. 'I made it sound like Nichols had cracked. In about an hour, Bob, call and tell him you've just got word from me Clampetti escaped. Say I particularly wanted him to know so he could protect himself.'

Captain Benton burst into the room. 'Hey,' he roared, 'there's a lead just came in on the Madison woman. Female answering her description checked in at the Lauderdale Hotel up Coast Highway about ten miles. Some highway patrolmen picked it up and passed it along. Seems the A.P.B. paid off.'

'We'll check it out,' Paul said. 'Don't forget about Mallory, Bob.'

'I won't, but what about Nichols?'

Paul faced back toward Benton. 'What's the

medic say?' he asked.

Benton smiled thinly. 'Nichols hasn't been hooked long enough for withdrawal to endanger his life.'

'Then make him a trade—Clampetti's whereabouts for the jolt. Call us in the car if he cracks.'

The drive up the Coast Highway was pleasant except for enormous trucks boring into the new day with thunderous motors roaring. They found the hotel with no effort, were pleased to discover its owner was a retired policeman.

'Yeah; I listened to a repeat of an A.P.B.', he told them. 'It's the same dame I'm pretty sure. A real looker—this heifer. Checked in after midnight sometime. Her car's around back. Someone's taken the registration slip off the steering column but not long ago; the column's clean as a whistle where the holder was.'

Pat jerked his head sideways. 'Check out the licence,' he said to Mike, 'just in case. I'll go wake her up.'

It was Golda Madison. She was frozen at sight of him in the doorway when the retired policeman unlocked the door, threw it wide and stepped back.

'Good morning.' He entered the room noting circles under her eyes. 'Why did you do it?'

She didn't reply until after the hotel owner

186

had closed the door and disappeared. 'I had to.'

He sat down holding his hat. 'That's a good reason—why?'

'I was afraid.'

'Police protection is better than flight,' he said. 'Suppose that man who phoned had been watching . . .'

'I wore a disguise.'

Paul spread his hands out. 'I found you—he could have also.'

'I need a drink.'

'Not this early in the day. Let's quit duelling, Miss Madison.'

'There's nothing I can tell you.'

'All right, I'll tell you, then. To start with you may not know *who* killed Drexler, but you know *why* he was killed. You and Mallory invested money with him. Mallory talked you into going along in it. When the investment went sour Mallory threatened Drexler who made good your losses, but it stuck in your mind that Drexler, whom you hadn't thought much of before, was more of a financial wizard than Mallory was. You jilted Mallory and became engaged to Drexler.'

'That's not true. My engagement to Pat was finished a year before Hugo and I became engaged.'

'All right; that's detail. The important thing is that Drexler showed Mallory up as an incompetent adviser—you told me yourself

Drexler was jealous of Mallory's capacity as your adviser. Mallory has been losing heavily on the market for some time; when Drexler not only became your fiancé but was on the verge of also becoming your confidant and adviser, Mallory couldn't take it. Drexler's mistake was in under-estimating Mallory, who is an egotist—he can't stand ridicule in any form, not any kind of a blow to his vanity. When Drexler made him look incompetent in your eyes he decided to kill him.'

'That's not so. Pat wouldn't kill anything—I told you that before. I know Pat Mallory better than to believe that of him.'

'I didn't say *Mallory* killed Drexler; I didn't mean Pat Mallory pulled the trigger. I'm like you—I don't believe he'd kill anyone—but I believe it for a different reason. I think he's too smart to commit murder. Nevertheless he planned Drexler's killing.'

'How?'

'He used the fact that the police department had a secret witness to the Gino Kapelli gang slaying—which happened in front of Drexler's apartment house—to plant the rumour that Drexler was that witness. Naturally, the gunman who murdered Kapelli had to try and protect himself by eliminating this witness. He shot Drexler.'

'That's preposterous.'

'Not altogether. Now—the sequel is what you probably don't know. Another rumour was spread in the underworld to the effect that Drexler hadn't been the secret witness after all, and that Mallory had only started his rumour in order to make certain that Kapelli's killer would murder Drexler. I'm certain you aren't aware that gangsters are even more sensitive about ridicule and being duped than Pat Mallory is. As soon as Kapelli's murderer heard how Mallory had used him, he set out to kill Mallory for revenge. One more killing doesn't worry a murderer, Miss Madison.'

'That's why Pat got that gun permit; that's why he wanted to know what the man I saw following me looked like.'

'That's only part of it. He also demanded police protection, and about three hours ago he found a listening device plugged into the telephone line at your apartment. I was there when he found it.'

'A listening device,' she said, large-eyed. 'Someone was listening to my telephone calls?'

'Yes; every call you made was monitored.'

Golda seemed to sink lower in the chair. 'Who did that?'

'The point is,' Paul said, side-stepping the answer, 'you are implicated in murder and the best thing for you to do is explain everything to me that you can about it.'

She persisted. 'That man . . . that dark man. But who *is* he?'

'I have only an idea. It may have been Clampetti, but if it was, why would he follow

189

you, and how did he know you were involved with Mallory? Was he tall or short?'

'Medium sized.'

'My size?'

'No, smaller and broader.'

'Then it wasn't Clampetti, which makes me think you imagined he was following you. Have you ever seen him around your apartment since that one night you went out and thought he was following you?'

'No, but you were there last night when I got the telephone call.'

'Miss Madison, that telephone call was *not* from a dark and heavy man. I know who made that call. I also know Mallory rigged up his perfect alibi by using an illegal emigrant to steal the car he reported missing. I know enough to prosecute you as an accessory to murder, and before this evening I'll have enough to arrest Mallory on the same charge. There's only one thing I don't know which I've *got* to know—the hiding place of Anthony Clampetti. If you know, I think the best thing you can do right now is tell me.'

'I don't know who this Anthony Clampetti is. I've never heard his name before and that's the truth.'

'But you did know that Mallory intended to kill Hugo Drexler.'

She shook her head vigorously. 'No, that's not so. I only knew Pat hated Hugo after Pat asked him for a tip on the market and Hugo gave him the one we both lost money on.'

'Do you mean to tell me he didn't once tell you, or hint to you, that he knew how Drexler happened to be killed?'

'I'm not going to answer that. I'm not going to tell you another thing.'

Mike Karger's entrance put a halt to the questioning. He nodded slightly at Golda and removed his hat just inside the door. 'Car's hers, it tallied-out. I called Bob—Nichols broke. They're waiting for us to come back in. Cap sent some squad cars down to make the surround.'

Paul stood up. 'Put your hat on, Miss Madison, you're under arrest on suspicion of being an accessory to murder.'

They drove back through town with the siren wailing. Golda sat low in the seat staring rigidly ahead. Mike was hunched over the back seat with a worried expression; Paul wove through traffic without slackening speed, jolted to a halt before headquarters and climbed out. Mike had Golda's arm as they went up steps, inside and across the vestibule to the booking desk. The officer on duty looked twice at Golda, rang a bell for a matron and watched Paul and Mike go down the hall towards Levin's office. Paul felt emptied. Captain Benton looked at him steadily for a moment after they entered and did not speak. Bob Levin held out a scrap of paper.

'The address,' he said. 'We've been in

contact. The squads have verified it's Clampetti all right from I.D. photos and the neighbours.'

'Not the neighbourhood I'd visualised,' Paul said handing the slip to Mike. 'Let's go.'

'You bring her in?' Benton said, arising.

'Yes.'

They spoke very little until Bob Levin parked down a grimy thoroughfare which had been temporarily closed off, traffic re-routed, by uniformed policemen. Mike counted four black-and-white patrol cars in sight, thought it likely an equal number were on the other approaches to the square and climbed out seeking the address and the right building. The morning was crisply cool and pleasant. The sun was still climbing and down at the far road-block a milkman was arguing with the uniformed policemen. It was still quite early.

Captain Benton was unwinding the cord to a loud-speaker and cursing each snarl. Bob Levin moved around to stand beside Mike.

'That brown brick place?'

Mike nodded. 'Paul? What's the pitch?'

'I'll go up like I did with Nichols.'

'The hell you will,' Benton said with the loud-speaker finally ready. 'I'll call him out; if he doesn't come—tear-gas.'

'Let me try first.'

'He'll shoot the first man he thinks is a cop, you ought to know that.'

'I also know something else; if we stir him

up and make a battle out of it he's going to get killed.'

Benton fed the insulated wire through his hand to a man in uniform who was plugging it into a scuffed black box on the ground. 'Better him than you,' he said, hefting the loud-speaker.

'Wait a minute,' Paul said swiftly. 'Let's at least make a try.'

Benton fidgeted, looked up squint-eyed at the old rooming-house a moment then gave his reluctant approval. Mike moved over beside Paul.

'I'll go up with you.'

'You and Bob'll go as far as the front entrance and wait there. If anything happens you'll hear it; then you'll come up.'

'Okay.'

The three of them moved toward the building. Distraught faces peered at them from behind windows. Back by the cars Captain Benton gave explicit orders. Uniformed policemen took position behind the cars with rifles and shot-guns, several had the peculiarly shaped and big-bored tear-gas carbines. Benton laid aside the loud-speaker long enough to call the other cars around the block and alert them, then he drew his service revolver—a .357 magnum with a very short barrel—and leaned across the bonnet of a car squinting upwards.

Mike and Bob stopped at the dingy door

and Paul kept on going. The hallway was rank with odours and gloomy. At a door bearing the legend manager he stopped and rapped. A smaller sign said 'No Peddlers —All Rooms Cash in Advance'. He had to knock twice more before a gross woman in late middle life opened the door with a sleep-fogged and ugly face made less pleasant by being awakened.

'Whatcha want?'

He held out the I.D. folder, moved it so the palest shaft of light coming from behind her fell across it. 'Police. How many tenants do you have?'

'How many? About nine.'

'Can you name them?'

'Well—which one you want?'

'Get your registry if you can't remember the names.'

'Sure, just a second.'

Paul put his foot in the door and listened to the flap of the woman's slippers. After a brief wait a hulking man appeared at the door clad in trousers and under-shirt.

'You a cop?'

Paul held out the folder showing his badge again and said, 'Where's your register-book?'

Still gazing drowsily at the badge the man held out a soiled piece of paper. 'The one without lines through 'em are still here. We get a big turn-over.'

Paul read the names but none rang a bell. He took out Clampetti's rap-sheet, unfolded it and held the little picture up. 'Which one is this?'

The man bent to peer, his breath was foul. 'That's Al Carter.'

'Good; the initials haven't changed. What's his room number?'

'Down the hall there. Room nine.'

'Does he have a telephone?'

'No; none of the rooms have—only ours.'

'All right; go on back to bed.'

Paul was moving away when the large man ran a nervous hand through his awry hair. 'Ain't going to be a beef in here, is there? I don't like trouble, officer.'

'Neither do I. The rest of it's up to Mr. Carter.' He waited until the big man had closed and bolted his door before continuing on down the hall. The door marked with a brass numeral nine appeared locked. Paul tried it very gently and found this to be true. He held his breath and listened. There wasn't a sound from the other side of the panel. Calling out would be suicide. He braced himself, swung sideways and threw his body against the door. It broke loose at the lock and slammed violently inwards. The shades were drawn and except for the weakest possible light from the murky hallway the room was pitch dark. He saw the man in the bed rise up and called out bleakly.

'Freeze, Clampetti. Don't make another move.'

The vague outline stopped moving. One hand was close to the edge of the bed where mattress and springs joined.

'Take your hand away from there. Put them up in the air. That's fine, now just stay like that.'

He moved closer to the bed from the far side. A little square on the wall drew his attention. Groping, he found the plastic lever and threw it. Light burst from twin lamps on either side of the bed. He had never seen Anthony Clampetti before in his life but it was a familiar face he saw now, with widening eyes wet from sleep, and a dark, oily countenance dominated by a crooked nose, lipless mouth and a pointed chin that thrust out.

'You're under arrest for murder. Keep your hands up full length and when I toss those covers back, get up.'

Anthony Clampetti obeyed if not meekly at least without protest or quick movements; Paul's service revolver fifteen inches from his head was a strong inducement to docility. He stood up and Paul moved around to stand on his right side.

'Walk. Go out into the hall and turn right. Don't lower your hands an inch or I'll kill you. Walk right out on to the sidewalk.'

Mike and Bob Levin were waiting. Mike drew Clampetti's arms down and held them while Bob Levin locked the cuffs behind Clampetti's back. Paul holstered his gun and returned to the disordered room, caught up Clampetti's clothing and a sturdy little overnight bag, plundered the closet and chifferobe, found nothing of interest and went back outside. A uniformed man took the clothing from him and headed for Bob Levin's car where Mike was talking to Captain Benton. Uniformed policemen swarmed up until Benton told them to get back on their beats and sent a similar order to the others around the square.

When the block had resumed a normal appearance Paul got into the car and twisted to gaze at Anthony Clampetti. Mike was helping the prisoner get dressed. Clampetti was white-faced, his mouth pulled back flat, and he hadn't said a word since Paul had awakened him. Benton wanted details, Paul gave them to him as Bob Levin edged in and started the car, pulled away from the kerb and edged out into the traffic.

At headquarters Clampetti was offered a plate of jail fare which he spurned with a snarled curse. 'What you guys think you're doing?'

'I told you once,' Paul said. 'You're under arrest for murder.'

'You're nuts, cop. Who did I murder, tell me?'

'Gino Kapelli to start with, then a man named Drexler—and finally, Detective Herb Rasch.'

'Where's your warrant for arresting me?'

Captain Benton held aloft a folded paper without speaking.

'Who says I murdered anybody?'

Bob Levin bent a little from the waist. 'We've got a secret witness who saw you blast Kapelli.'

'Secret witness my neck. You guys got nothing—nothing at all, damn your lousy hides. Get me a phone. I'll have my lawyer down here in ten minutes.'

'Your lawyer'll be down here all right.'

'Get me a phone. You can't hold me without legal counsel. I know my rights, you lead-bottoms.'

Captain Benton stood up stiffly. 'One more wise crack,' he said, 'and you'll need a doctor not a lawyer —remember that!'

They exchanged hostile stares and Clampetti looked away. 'Get me a phone,' he said again.

'Better get the booking officer, Mike.' After Mike went out the door Paul faced the killer again. 'Would you like to know who tipped us off, Clampetti; a friend of yours named Marty—Marty Nichols.'

'I don't know nobody named Marty Nichols—what you think of that?'

'Would you like to know? I think you're a damned liar, and I can prove it.'

'You can't hold me without—'

'Here,' Mike said from the doorway. 'His

198

name's Anthony Clampetti. Book him for murder.'

The registration officer went to Levin's desk and shot questions. Paul watched a moment then went across the hall to an empty office strong with the odour of cigars and telephoned Patrick Mallory.

'We've got Miss Madison down here if you'd like to see her. Just picked her up a little while ago.' When Mallory said he'd be right down Paul hung up, lit a cigarette and sauntered back to Bob Levin's office. Captain Benton was ripping into the killer with fired questions. Clampetti was grimly silent except for an occasional demand that he be allowed to call his lawyer. Paul glanced at his watch and after a while nodded his head.

'Go ahead; here's the phone.'

Clampetti dialled a number which did not answer. He gripped the instrument harder and dialled another number. Still he drew no answer, then, just as he was preparing to hang up, a quietly disturbed and elderly voice came down the line. Clampetti's head jerked forward.

'Lemme talk to Mallory and quick.'

Paul watched the dark face as the answer came back. Clampetti moved back and swore blisteringly into the instrument and slammed it down. 'He wasn't home, was he?' Paul said. 'Well, don't worry, he'll be here in a few minutes. I already called him.' He took Mike and Captain Benton to one side, spoke shortly and sat down at Levin's desk when they left the room. The silence built up. Clampetti shot lowering glares at Bob who was smoking and leaning on the wall, and Paul Brewster who was regarding him steadily. Finally he shattered the stillness with a hoarse curse.

'Just because I got a record—'

'Shut up!'

Clampetti closed his mouth hard. Moments went by. Someone was coming up the corridor. Behind the first set of footfalls there were others. Clampetti glued his eyes to the opening hopefully and Paul was watching him. When Mike Karger led Marty Nichols by Clampetti started in his chair. When Golda Madison and Captain Benton went by, Clampetti only looked puzzled. There was no spark of recognition. Paul lit a cigarette satisfied that the man Golda Madison thought had been following her was pure imagination.

A siren went off down in the street. Clampetti's jaw muscles quivered. He squirmed on his chair. 'When's Mallory coming?' he asked.

'He'll be along. How long have you known him?'

'Mallory? I don't know the guy at all. Just heard around town he's a smart lawyer.'

' "How smart? Smart enough to start that rumour about Drexler being our secret witness so you'd knock him off?'

'Man,' Clampetti said in protest, 'you've slipped a cog. Who's this Drexler anyway?'

'The fellow you killed in the apartment on Fairfax; the man Mallory spread the rumour was our secret witness so you would kill him. Mallory sure used you on that, Clampetti.'

'You're a mixed-up guy, Brewster. Real mixed up, man.'

'Am I? How about the story of you being after Mallory? That's been circulating around town for a week.'

'Me? After Mallory? I told you, I don't even know the man.'

'Hell,' Paul said dryly, 'you didn't know Drexler either. That didn't stop you from throwing a blast into him. You want some advice, Clampetti? Turn State's evidence before Mallory does. He's an attorney, knows all the legal angles. He knows, for instance, that he can get off pretty clean—get a light sentence—if he co-operates with the D.A. You're a mug, an uneducated hoodlum. You wouldn't be expected to know that if he testifies for the State against you—he'll get off easy and you'll get Death Row.'

'What could he testify against me about?' Clampetti said, genuinely perplexed. 'He don't know me and I don't know him.'

'He can testify how he engineered Drexler's killing. We have enough evidence on the Kapelli murder to tie you up solid. All Mallory's got to do is explain how he out-smarted you—made you believe Drexler was the police department's secret witness so you'd murder him.'

'Man; that's far-fetched. Who'd buy that anyway? A jury? In a pig's eye, Brewster. You're trying to make a case and it stinks, brother—it's pure garbage.'

'Drexler wasn't our witness, Clampetti. Our secret witness, the man who actually saw you shoot Kapelli, is downstairs in the tanks right this minute. He's signed an affidavit identifying you. He'll swear under oath in court you shot and killed Kapelli.'

'More garbage,' Clampetti scoffed.

Paul opened Bob Levin's top drawer, flipped back the folder on top and sifted through documents until he found the one he sought. He held it up. 'Read the first paragraph of that. Never mind the signature, just the first paragraph.' Clampetti's dark, muddy eyes raced over the words. Paul put the affidavit back into the folder. 'Satisfied,' he said. 'You thought it was all malarkey, didn't you? It isn't and never was. We've got a witness that'll put you to death, Clampetti. We've also got other witnesses—not on the Kapelli killing but on other aspects of this case. Nichols fingered Detective Rasch for you. That was the most senseless and stupid killing you ever committed. You could have slid out the back way but no, you're a real hot torpedo, you aren't afraid of the law, no cop can make you sneak away. Cop-killers don't last long in this town, Clampetti. You've had it on that account, believe me.'

'Where is that damned shyster,' Clampetti snarled. 'You was lying. You didn't call him.'

'I called him, don't worry, he'll be along, but I don't think he'll represent you. Coming back to the point I'm trying to get across to you— the only chance you've got on the Drexler rap is to turn State's evidence before Mallory does, and if you'd take advice, Clampetti, I wouldn't advise you to hire a lawyer to represent you who is going to be prosecuted as an accessory for the same murder, for two reasons. One, he won't be able to appear for you in court. Two, if he could, he'd get you executed to save his own neck; he'd toss you to the lions just like he tossed his friend Drexler.'

'You're going to arrest Mallory?' Clampetti asked with a narrowed stare.

'That's right; as soon as he walks in this door I'm going to arrest him as an accessory to murder,' Paul replied. 'Maybe you're wising up. You know darned well what he'll do as soon as he's booked and interrogated. He'll offer to make a deal with the State to give evidence against the man who did the actual killing—you.'

'How? Saying I killed this mug Drexler— how could Mallory be a witness against me? Saying I blasted the guy—did Mallory see me do it?'

Paul shook his head. 'No, *he* didn't, but our secret witness did.'

'So how could Mallory burn me?'

'By testifying for us that he deliberately started the story about Drexler being our witness knowing you'd try to kill him before he could be made to testify in court against you. That makes Mallory an accessory—see? He could have been ten thousand miles away, Clampetti, and if he encouraged the murder of another person the law says he is just as guilty as the man who actually pulled the trigger. You may not know that much law but Mallory does. He also knows if he gives evidence for the prosecution he won't get the maximum penalty—only you will get that.'

Clampetti reached for a packet of cigarettes on Levin's desk with his manacled hands, had trouble lighting one and cursed. Paul held out his lighter. Clampetti sucked in a big lungful of smoke, held it a second and expelled it. 'I got to get another lawyer,' he said finally. 'I don't believe half what you said, Brewster, but if you're going to drag Mallory I got to get another shyster.'

'At least that much soaked in,' Paul said. 'You're going to get one hell of a surprise when you go into court, too. We've built up a very good case against you and Mallory.'

'Real good, huh?' Clampetti said, staring at Paul from his squinted eyes.

'It had to be good. We've got to be sure too;

Mallory's going to do his damndest to beat this rap. Getting the evidence hasn't been like dealing with a hood, Clampetti. Attorneys know more law than cops.'

'Yeah,' Clampetti said through smoke.

Mike and Captain Benton entered the room and not far behind them came Bob Levin. He passed a note to Paul who read it, folded it and pocketed it without any change in his expression. Benton stood squarely in the centre of the office with his legs slightly apart. None of them spoke and Clampetti kept his glance off their faces. Paul arose, glanced at his watch and wrinkled his forehead.

'I'm going down to the tanks. If Mallory doesn't show up in another ten minutes call the stake-out.'

'I already did,' Benton said. 'He said Mallory left the house and he put one of the other lads to tailing him.'

Paul walked out into the corridor. Mike followed him until they were beyond Clampetti's earshot. 'What's next—did he recognise them?'

'He recognised Nichols all right, but not Golda.'

'Nichols recognised him too,' Mike said. 'When I took him back downstairs he said he'd give a statement.'

'Were we right?'

'Right as rain. As soon as the rumour came around about Clampetti getting Mallory,

Nichols got a call from Mallory to tell Clampetti it was a trap—that he didn't know Drexler and hadn't set him up for Clampetti to kill. Nichols said he never got a chance to pass it along, we picked him up before he met Clampetti again.'

'What about Herb?'

'Nichols said he didn't know Herb but when he was coming to work late that afternoon he saw a plain-clothes cop park his department car a couple blocks down from the Aloha. Herb walked toward the club so Nichols followed him. When Herb took up a position across the street Nichols said he knew damned well what Herb was up to; when he went inside and saw Clampetti at the bar he warned him. Clampetti had been drinking and he told Nichols no damned cop alive could take him, and walked outside.'

'And that's how Herb got it.'

'Just like that. What's next?'

'Mallory ought to be along shortly. I'm going down and talk to Golda; that note was from her. When Mallory gets here call me downstairs.'

'Do we let him talk to Clampetti?'

'We can't stop him, it's the law, but I don't think Clampetti's going to be too friendly toward him. Ask Bob to turn on his desk recorder as soon as Mallory comes in, I want to hear what they say to each other, Mallory and Clampetti.'

'What's Clampetti got to say about Herb?'

'I didn't press that, Mike. Look; Mallory was just as indirectly responsible for Herb's murder as he was for Drexler's. Let's concentrate on nailing him first. Afterwards we'll sweat it out of Clampetti about Herb, don't worry.'

He went downstairs, picked up a matron at the female detention tank office, went down the row of cells until he found Golda's. She crossed toward him and he noticed that even in the pale blue denim dress she was lovely. His face was a mask hiding pain.

'I got your note.'

'Thanks for coming,' Golda said in a subdued tone looking into his face. 'I want to request that Pat be notified I'm here.'

'He already knows. I called him about a quarter of an hour ago.' He expected her eyes to brighten; they didn't.

'If you still want me to I'm ready to make a statement.'

'I'm glad,' he said. 'It'll help you at your trial.'

'Mr. Brewster—will I be sent to prison?"

'I can't say. We turn the evidence over to the District Attorney's office; they prosecute.' He wanted to reach through the bars and pat her shoulder. 'Could I give you some advice?'

'I'd be grateful if you would.'

'Request a meeting with the prosecuting attorney—his name is Corte. Tell him everything you know; don't hide anything at all. If what you say can be used to help the State make their case Corte may offer to go light on you.'

'Do you mean incriminate Pat?'

He nodded without answering. She looked past him at the matron and back again. Her hand on the bars dropped to her side and she started to turn away.

'Miss Madison; answer me truthfully: Did you know that Mallory planned to get Drexler killed?'

'No. All I really knew was what Pat told me afterwards. He said Hugo had asked for it; that Hugo had antagonised the wrong man. From that I knew Pat had something to do with the killing. Later, after you had called, I asked Pat exactly what he'd done and he told me he'd out-smarted Drexler and the underworld; he was proud of it and boasted a little. Then he told me if I breathed a word of what he'd said I'd be implicated with him. That's the exact truth, Mr. Brewster.'

Paul regarded her levelly for a moment of silence, then he said, 'I hope it is. I hope for your sake it is, because if you tell Mr. Corte that, and he believes it's the truth, I don't think you'll be prosecuted, but don't get heroic, Miss Madison; don't try to shield Mallory. If you do you won't be able to save him and you'll definitely hurt your own chances.'

A matron came up and told him Mike

Karger had called and said Mr. Mallory was upstairs. He nodded and turned back to Golda Madison. 'If there's anything I can do, let me know.'

'I appreciate that,' she said, and smiled at him. 'I don't suppose you know what it's like to lead a purposeless life, do you?'

'I'm not sure I know what you mean, Miss Madison.'

'Well; to have no purpose—no goal.'

'Yes,' he said, 'I can understand that, I guess, but I've never felt that way,' and he smiled at her. 'I never had the chance, I've had to work all my life.'

'Thank you for coming down.' He had turned away when she spoke again. 'Those were good waffles, too.'

He had no trouble understanding her meaning. 'Yes, they were,' he said, and walked away.

Upstairs Levin's little office seemed crammed with people. Captain Benton's personality was projecting itself throughout the room in an acrimonious exchange with Patrick Mallory whose face was red and angry looking. Paul caught Mike's significant nod as he passed through the door. Bob Levin was standing with his hands in his pockets near Clampetti's chair. His face was cold and unfriendly. Mallory was speaking.

'You people've been trying to make a case for over a week now, and you've done nothing

209

but confuse an issue which should have been open and closed.'

Benton started to deny that when Paul interrupted him. 'Mr. Mallory; I know you don't think much of policemen. You've made that obvious since the first time I met you, but there's a saying about underestimating the enemy and I believe you've done it.'

Mallory turned his head, fixed hostile eyes on Paul and said, 'Brewster; I wandered how long it'd be before you came in. Where's Miss Madison?'

'She's downstairs in the tanks,' Paul replied, and spoke aside to Mike. 'Call Corte at the D.A.'s office and ask him to come over, will you?' When Mike left the room Paul spoke directly to Mallory. 'You've heard of the perfect alibi, haven't you?' When Mallory refused to reply Paul said, 'You had it, Mallory. You had the perfect alibi. When you were down here reporting that stolen car at the time Drexler was being killed you established the fact very neatly that you couldn't have murdered him.'

'No one ever said I did murder him, Brewster.'

'I'm saying it now, Mallory. In fact, as of this moment you are under arrest for being an accessory to Drexler's murder.'

'You're insane.'

'If you'd pulled the trigger you wouldn't be any more guilty. We know how you planned and engineered that killing; why you drove to headquarters to report the car theft. We also have the man in custody whom you paid one thousand dollars to for stealing your car.'

'I can pay anyone any amount I wish to drive my car anywhere and do anything with it so long as I'm violating no law.'

'True. You make a good point, Mallory, only you can't have your own car stolen to conceal participation in a felony without being prosecuted for doing it. Another thing, when you threatened Golda Madison and bragged how you'd out-smarted Clampetti here—got him to kill Drexler in such a way that you wouldn't be involved—you made another mistake. She's agreed to give us an affidavit to that effect—tell us exactly what you told her. The mistake you made there is part of your character; you had to prove to her that you were smarter than Drexler after all. You had to erase the humiliation he'd caused you when he made you look like a fool in front of her on a bad investment.' Mallory opened his mouth to speak. Paul made a gesture to cut him off and kept on talking.

'Another blunder you made was when you used Marty Nichols the hophead as your underworld contact. Nichols would sell his soul for heroin, he sold us something much better than a junkie's soul—information about how you tried to contact Clampetti when you heard he was after you for duping him into killing

211

Drexler.'

Mallory shot Clampetti a look. 'He's making this up to sucker you into testifying for him,' he said. 'Don't fall for it.'

Paul said, 'Clampetti, when you're dead to save Mallory's neck he'll be laughing at you. Mallory, if you'd called that car theft in we might have strung along—maybe we wouldn't have tumbled at all—so the perfect alibi itself was what tripped you up. Cops are dumb; probably much dumber than attorneys—at least not as well educated—but there's something you over-looked. When a crime is committed the criminal has done something he can't go back and do over. The police can take their time; nothing's going to change the crime; they can dig and probe and question until they find out what happened—how it happened—and who did it. The actual advantage lies with the police and not even a smart lawyer can go back and cover up his mistakes.'

'I warned you once, Brewster. Now I'll warn you again; everything you've said so far, even if it were true, is nothing but circumstantial evidence. If I'd planned Drexler's murder as you say, it still couldn't be verified by anything stronger than surmise. You ought to know the law deals only in facts. If you went to court with what you have the case would be thrown out and I'd sue the city. The Commissioner would be out of his head to allow a thing like

212

this to come to court. I don't believe he'd do it.'

Paul held up his hand, fingers closed. 'Golda Madison's affidavit,' he said, and raised one finger. 'That definitely ties you to the murder by your own admission. The faked car theft and the man you paid to steal the car—he has already identified you, Mallory. That's number two. An audit of your bank account, Miss Madison's and Hugo Drexler's proves you and Miss Madison invested with Drexler, lost, and were reimbursed. That's another tie-in. Your broken romance and Miss Madison's accounts of your character, the way you boasted to her about the Drexler murder. That's number four. Those will do us for a starter. We've got quite a bit more. When Mike and I first went on this case we knew how careful and how positive we'd need to be to bring you to trial. We wouldn't be arresting you now if we didn't know we had enough evidence to get a conviction. The District Attorney's office worked with us. They know as much law as you do, Mallory.'

Mallory's face was pale and blanked over. He stared at Paul in absolute silence. Before he spoke Corte walked in. He was carrying a pale brown briefcase and his quick glance darted around the room, came to rest on Paul's face; he nodded. Captain Benton caught his arm, led him to a far corner and the sound of their voices was low, like the hum of bees.

'If you try this,' Mallory said. 'I'll institute counter-suit against the city.'

Paul gestured towards the telephone on Bob Levin's desk. 'Then you'd better call an attorney,' he said, 'because we're going through with it.' He looked across at Mallory. 'But there's something you might do to save your neck. You might turn State's evidence, tell how you worked Drexler's killing and get off light.'

There was scorn in the attorney's face but when he was ready to reply Anthony Clampetti burst in. 'Hold on,' he said to Paul. 'You can't do that—you already offered to let me get my licks in first.'

Mallory turned slowly and gazed down at the prisoner. 'Are you insane,' he said. 'Neither one of us have to turn State's evidence.'

'Don't we,' Clampetti snarled at him. 'You wise bastard you—getting someone else to do your dirty work. I wish I *had* got you, shyster; I wish there'd been something to that talk about me gunning for you. You sure got me in the side-pocket didn't you? You don't pull it off now though—not by a damned sight.'

'You idiot; there's absolutely nothing to tie me to you or you to me. If you killed Drexler you did it on your own—I had nothing whatsoever to do with it. There isn't a shred of proof and if you're smart you'll deny it no matter what anyone says.'

'No proof, you louse? Why, Marty Nichols

himself told me you said Drexler was the guy.'

Paul looked at Mike in surprise. They both turned to watch Clampetti whose face was swollen and dark with anger.

'You told Marty you *knew* this Drexler was the finger.'

'That's a lie,' Mallory said. Before he could say anything more Corte walked toward the desk, put his brief-case upon it and spoke to Mallory.

'I think this discussion has been informal up to now, Mr. Mallory, but you ought to be warned that whatever you say can be offered as evidence against you.'

Mallory straightened up, appraised Corte, then said, 'You surely aren't going to prosecute on what they have, are you?'

'You don't know all they have, Mr. Mallory. Yes, we're going to prosecute.'

'The best you can hope for is an accessory conviction.'

'We'll settle for that. A felony-murder accessory conviction could put you away for life.'

Mallory became silent. Captain Benton moved back into the centre of the room and lit a cigarette. The rasp of his lighter was the only sound until Bob Levin reached over and touched Clampetti's shoulder. The prisoner, staring hatred at Patrick Mallory, started in the chair.

'You want to dictate a statement?' Levin

215

asked quietly.

'Sure.' He looked around at Corte. 'I'm volunteering to testify for the prosecution about the Drexler case. Okay?'

Corte's face was impassive. He nodded his head. 'Yes; in exchange we'll ask only life imprisonment. Is that what you want?'

'Right,' Clampetti said.

Levin looked at Captain Benton with raised eyebrows. Benton said, 'Take him across the hall and get a stenographer to take it down.'

When Clampetti and Levin left Paul lit a cigarette, offered Mike one, got a refusal and pocketed the pack. 'There went your chance,' he said to Mallory.

'That damned fool's talking himself into the morgue,' Mallory said.

Paul agreed. 'Sure he is, but not on the Drexler rap. The State will ask consideration for co-operation—a life stretch instead of the maximum penalty of death. You heard him make the offer and Mr. Corte's acceptance. We'll keep faith with him on that count.'

'And the others?'

'He'll get Death Row for the Rasch killing but right now he's so busy hating you he doesn't realise that. There's never been a cop-killer turned loose in this city.'

'Has he got a good lawyer?' Mallory asked.

'He hasn't any right now, that I know of. When we brought him in he wanted to hire you. After I told him you wouldn't be around to represent him—and a few other things—he soured on you but good.'

'That's defamation of character,' Mallory said without much conviction.

Paul pushed out the cigarette. 'Sue me on it,' he said. '*After* your trial. Better book him, Mike.' He got up and gazed at Benton. Neither of them spoke until Mallory was out of the room then Paul said, 'It's up to the jury; *we're* satisfied he's guilty as hell.'

Corte sat on the edge of the desk idly swinging his leg. 'Will the Madison woman give us a statement?'

'She said she would about an hour ago. Corte, she's not an accomplice.'

'No? What did you book her for?'

'No charge, protective custody.'

'I'll talk to her.'

'Give her a break. She's going to level with you.'

Corte looked up. 'All right; if I can,' he said watching Paul's face.

'Thanks,' Paul said as Benton crossed to Clampetti's vacated chair and sank down into it.

'After you make a study of the evidence let me know what Mallory's chances are,' he said to Corte.

'I can tell you this much from what I've already read of the charges; he'll get life or fifty-years-to-life. I'm not at all worried about him; the guy I'd like to tear into is that

217

Clampetti character. He's a sure-fire conviction for Death Row. Our office likes cases like that.'

'Be plenty of publicity,' Benton said dourly. 'It'll make the D.A. look good for the primaries, won't it?'

Corte nodded his head. Paul looked at them both for a moment then went toward the door. The corridor was empty but there was sound in it; teletypes clicking and clattering not far away, the drone of men's voices, sounds of police activity. He walked down toward the staircase but at the last moment he stopped, rested his hand on the railing and didn't go down. There was nothing more to say. He would watch her end of the case anyway. He thought of the others. Sabellis would come out clean; it was too bad he had to get wrung out like that but a criminal record is never buried. And that witness—that guy from the delicatessen—he had probably lost ten pounds already; he'd lose another five pounds during the trial. Nichols? The D.A. would ask for a commitment for him to a State institution; it might work; when they weren't hooked any worse than he was sometimes they straightened up, shook it off; not often but sometimes. What else was there? Benton's talk of promotion. It left him unmoved. His fingers tapped on the railing. A good case for the Commissioner. That made his lips turn down a little; Herb Rasch's family living on a half-pay pension. Loose ends, details, minutae; every case had them; human beings, lives torn out by the roots, twisted and flung away—some, like Clampetti—being fed into the never-filled maw of justice; being ground up and dissolved into nothing.

He stared down the lighted stair-well. A faint odour of antiseptic came up to him. No purpose in life . . . One engagement after another . . . drifting . . . comfort, wealth, beauty and no purpose. He gripped the railing.

'Paul?'

He turned, watched Mike's heavy, thick body move toward him. Waited until he was up close then took his hand off the railing.

'Aren't you going to eat? It's three o'clock.'

'That late,' Paul said absently, mildly surprised but not especially hungry. 'Yeah. How'd you make out with Clampetti?'

'Better than I expected. He's so bent on dragging Mallory in I had to watch him on the perjury angle. I'll tell you over lunch, come on.'

'Well; suppose you go on across and get us a table. Order me roast beef and coffee—and apple pie. I'll be over in a little while.'

Mike's eyes drifted from the face opposite him to the stair-well and back again. 'Sure,' he said, and walked away.

Footfalls echoed harshly on the descent. Paul had never noticed it before and he'd made the same trip hundreds of times. The tanks were divided at the bottom landing. On one side of a massively thick cement wall were the male prisoners, on the opposite side the female prisoners. A uniformed jailer touched his cap to Paul and a matron looked up from her desk and smiled. She was sorting file cards. Beyond, the long corridor was lighted as brightly as daylight by shielded fluorescent tubes. He glimpsed pale blue denim moving here and there. The matron watched his face.

'Recreation hour,' she said affably. 'That new one you brought in is the prettiest woman I've ever seen down here.'

'Prettiest woman I ever saw—period,' he said.

'She didn't go out; do you want to see her?'

He nodded and the matron arose, started down the lighted corridor. He moved after her and the jailer craned his neck to watch. He was an older man with a face pitted and seamed by the hardships and adventures of life. Something moved in his eyes; something like an inkling of a suspicion, and he smiled to himself as Paul stopped before a cell mid-way down the corridor.

1	21	41	61	81	101	121	141	161	181
2	22	42	62	82	102	122	142	162	182
3	23	43	63	83	103	123	143	163	183
4	24	44	64	84	104	124	144	164	184
5	25	45	65	85	105	125	145	165	185
6	26	46	66	(86)	106	126	146	166	186
7	27	47	67	87	107	127	147	167	187
8	28	48	68	88	108	128	148	168	188
9	29	49	69	89	109	129	149	169	189
10	30	50	70	90	110	130	150	170	190
11	31	51	71	91	111	131	151	171	191
12	32	52	72	92	112	132	152	172	192
13	33	53	73	93	113	133	153	173	193
14	34	54	74	94	114	134	154	174	194
15	35	55	75	95	115	135	155	175	195
16	36	56	76	96	116	136	156	176	196
17	37	57	77	97	117	137	157	177	197
18	38	58	78	98	118	138	158	178	198
19	39	59	79	99	119	139	159	179	199
20	40	60	80	100	120	140	160	180	200

201	216	231	246	261	276	291	306	321	336
202	217	232	247	262	277	292	307	322	337
203	218	233	248	263	278	293	308	323	338
204	219	234	249	264	279	294	309	324	339
205	220	235	250	265	280	295	310	325	340
206	221	236	251	266	281	296	311	326	341
207	222	237	252	267	282	297	312	327	342
208	223	238	253	268	283	298	313	328	343
209	224	239	254	269	284	299	314	329	344
210	225	240	255	270	285	300	315	330	345
211	226	241	256	271	286	301	316	331	346
212	227	242	257	272	287	302	317	332	347
213	228	243	258	273	288	303	318	333	348
214	229	244	259	274	289	304	319	334	349
215	230	245	260	275	290	305	320	335	350